ENVIOUS MOON

ALSO BY THOMAS CHRISTOPHER GREENE

I'll Never Be Long Gone

Mirror Lake

ENVIOUS MOON

THOMAS CHRISTOPHER GREENE

wm WILLIAM MORROW *An Imprint of* HarperCollins*Publishers*

HarperCollins books may be purchased for educational, business, or sales promotional use. For information please write: Special Markets Department, HarperCollins Publishers, 10 East 53rd Street, New York, NY 10022.

FIRST EDITION

Designed by Susan Yang

Library of Congress Cataloging-in-Publication Data

Greene, Thomas Christopher, 1968–
  Envious moon : a novel / Thomas Christopher Greene. — 1st ed.
    p. cm.
  ISBN: 978-0-06-115387-7
  ISBN-10: 0-06-115387-7
    I. Rhode Island—Fiction. I. Title.

PS3607.R453E58 2007
813'.6—dc22

                                        2006046757

---

07 08 09 10 11 DT/RRD 10 9 8 7 6 5 4 3 2 1

For Sarah

Acknowledgments

With gratitude, I would like to thank the following:

My talented editor, Jennifer Pooley. Also at Morrow: Lisa Gallagher, Kevin Callahan, and Ben Bruton. I truly appreciate everything you do in publishing my work.

My agent and friend, Nick Ellison, and his terrific colleagues, Sarah Dickman and Marissa Matteo.

My early readers: Maura Greene, Daniel Greene, David Greene, Susan McCarthy, Jennifer O'Connor, Margaret Gendron, Judith Austin, Alex Lehmann, and Big Al Donovan.

Dr. Susan O'Doherty, who provided professional advice about psychology and the mental health system.

My parents, for their remarkable support. And my wife, Tia, my first editor, my best friend, the reader whose opinions matter to me above all others'.

And finally, to my daughter, Sarah, to whom this book is dedicated. At six months old she cannot yet read my words. But her smile when she sees me would not only make the moon envious, it makes me want to write down every story I know, so that when she is old enough to read them, they will always be there.

I confess that sometimes I forget what she looks like. This upsets me. It doesn't last for long, though, and lately I've developed a trick. I anchor myself in her freckles, those lovely freckles that covered her cheeks, and then I see her eyes, and her hair, and soon all of her comes into focus. Dr. Mitchell says this is a good sign, my forgetting. It means it's time to move on, Anthony. You're still a young man, he says. The funny thing is that at first they spend all this time having you remember everything. Go over every detail and then suddenly they don't want to talk about it anymore. They want you to think about the future. They'll tell you they believe in memory but the truth is they don't. They want you to erase all that now. It's such a big world out there, Anthony, they say. It could all be yours again. It could all be yours.

I was born in Galilee, Rhode Island, that small spit of land jut-ting out into the Atlantic Ocean. My father used to say our house faced Portugal, which is where he was from. My mother, too, though they met in Galilee. My father's name was Rodrigo and he was a fisherman. My mother's name was Berta and for years she cooked at a small college in Westerly. I was an only child. There was one who came after me, a little sister, Marta, but she lived for less than a week. I was two when that hap-pened so I don't remember it. But I know it had a strong effect on both my parents. They told me later that I spent most of her one week of life just staring at her in her crib. Every year we celebrated her birthday as if she had been a normal sister, someone I had known.

We lived in a small bungalow in a neighborhood of small bungalows built by fishermen for fishermen. Houses painted bright colors but built on cinder blocks with small fenced-in yards. Almost everyone who lived in Galilee made their living from the sea and in our neighborhood everyone was also Por-tuguese. My earliest memories are all about the ocean. We had only a small sandy yard and so the harbor and the commercial wharves, the beaches and the inlets, the tidal streams and rivers, were my playground. My father fished on commercial boats and was often gone for as long as a month at a time during the season. My mother rose early to cook breakfast for college students. My best friend, Victor Perez, who lived one street away, and I were our own keepers. As small boys we swam in the tidal river on warm days, leaping off the bridge that crossed it. We fished off the rocky beach and by seven I could gut a fish by myself. We were from poor families and were expected to work, so we did what we could. We delivered newspapers and shoveled snow in the winter. We washed down decks of boats. Stacked wood. Dug clams out of the tidal flats and brought them in buckets down to Teagan's Seafood. And when my father was in between trips, he'd bring the two of us out at night on his small skiff to fish for blues and stripers. He'd lean against the gunwale and roll his own cigarettes and teach us everything he knew about fishing. He liked to talk and he liked to tell stories. My father was tall and handsome with thick hair and a prominent mustache. He had a quick temper but also a quick wit and he was my hero. Victor's too, I think. Victor's father drank and Victor spent as little time as he could at home. He was always at my house and I considered him a brother. As did my parents. And those times on the skiff are some of my most treasured memories. I wanted to be a man like my father. Roll my own cigarettes and wear my jeans tucked into mud boots. Have strong veiny forearms and a good mustache. Piercing brown eyes. Tell stories like he did.

The summer I turned ten my father got a new job on the *Mavis*, a swordboat. Swordfishing was the most lucrative of the commercial fishing jobs and that was a good summer and he made good money. We ate steak on nights he returned and listened to Red Sox games on the radio. The happiest nights of my life were the nights when he came home. We never knew when to expect him because a fishing boat only returns when it is full of fish or out of fuel. But somehow I could sense when he was on land. I don't know how to describe it and maybe it was just luck. But he was never able to surprise us. I'd stand in the front yard and watch the street and think, he's going to turn the corner now. It was like I was willing him to be there. And on those moments when I was right, I'd see him in the distance in the summer heat, at first only a figure outlined against the hot day. But there was no mistaking him, his walk. I'd run out to the street to him, yelling his name and when I got close, he'd stop and wait for me. He'd hold his arms out wide and smile. I'd jump into his arms and smell his cigarettes and all the fish he had caught. His sweat. He'd hold me up and kiss my cheeks and then put me down and tell me to get my mother. And it didn't matter how tired he was, we'd still spend hours kicking a soccer ball back and forth in the road. He'd tell me stories about life at sea. I wanted nothing more than to be on a boat with him. To learn to fish as he did and sometimes when I told him this, his mood changed. You won't be a fisherman, Anthony, he said.

My father always took the time to tell me how proud he was of me. Especially with how I did in school. I was a straight-A student from elementary school through junior high. They put me in a college-track program. I was the only son of a fisherman in those classes. That made my father prouder than anything. He taped my report cards to the refrigerator and he told all the men he worked with how smart his Anthony was. He used to tell me how I was going to go to a big college and then leave Galilee. I didn't like when he said this because I could not imagine leaving Galilee. He always said I was going to go to New York, and live in a big house and drive a nice car and marry a pretty woman and have kids who had a better life than I had. It should be easier for each generation, he said. That's our job as parents. I wanted to ask him: but what if I don't want to leave Galilee? What's wrong with my life? What if I want nothing more than to be like you? To fish with other men and when on land to kick a soccer ball with my son and eat steaks and listen to baseball?

But I never said these things to him. I knew how happy my report cards made him. I knew how pleased he was when my eighth-grade teacher, Mr. Loomis, called my parents to tell them that I was reading on a college level already. He told them that I could do whatever I wanted to do, and that college was within my sights if I kept working at it.

In 1984, I turned fourteen. This was in July and my father

was on the *Mavis* and they were fishing a seam in a roiling sea at night. It was their fourth night in a row and they pulled sword after sword and even with the high seas, to a man they did not wish to be anywhere else. At the rate they were going, each crewman might walk away with five grand. My father and another fisherman were at the bait table. They stood across from each other and as the line unfurled from the spool they took squid off the table and baited them on the big hooks. It was repetitive and hard work as there was no slowing down the line. But my father was a good fisherman and he was especially good at slapping the bait up there and catching it solid. Later other fishermen would tell me he almost never wasted a single hook.

At one point the men on the other side of the deck doing the butchering called for help, and the man across from my father left. My father was all alone and normally this would not have mattered since he was certainly fast enough to keep up on his own. But in the roiling sea the boat lurched suddenly to port and my father was thrown forward with the squid in his hand. The hook meant for the squid drove through the part of his palm where the thumb met the forefinger. In the whip of the wind whatever cries he might have made were drowned out. He was swept into the black sea.

If he had not been hooked so solidly, they may never have found him. They pulled him out of the icy Atlantic like a fish.

That night men from the co-op came to the house and I woke when I heard my mother's grief. It was a sound like no other. In the days that followed, everything slowed down. The house was always full of visitors and our small dining room table was covered with more food than we could ever eat. They held a wake at O'Brien's Funeral Home, in the small upstairs room they used for the poor people. The fishermen and their wives all came to pay their respects, and the fishermen looked like men who had no business being inside. I stood in the corner, and no one paid any attention to me, which was good because I refused to take my eyes off my father's body. My mother told me his soul would rise to heaven and I didn't want to miss it. I thought it would look like candle smoke, floating toward the ceiling. Though I didn't see anything. Later I figured it must have risen while he was still in the ocean.

After everyone had left, my mother kneeled in front of my father and said her good-byes. She wore black from head to toe and I remember that she had a run up one leg of her stockings. My mother spoke in Portuguese and she spoke in English and the words were meant for my father and not for me. But I knew, even at that young age I knew, that the words she spoke were words of love.

She spoke for a long while. And while she whispered to him she reached up and pushed her hands through his thick hair. She cupped his lifeless face in her hands. And that night, for the first time, I saw my parents as separate people. As Berta and as Rodrigo, a man and a woman who had loved one another. And I knew that the sea had taken my father. That the sea took many things. But that it could not take their love. Even after he was gone, the love remained. It was in the upstairs room of the funeral home that night. And for as long as I stayed in the small bungalow, it was in that house. I saw it in my mother's eyes.

After the funeral, I told my mother I was a man now and she didn't laugh at me. I said I would go to sea, and she said, "There will be plenty of time for that."

We went on. In the years that followed I grew tall and strong like my father. I had his curly hair and his big brown eyes. I hung around the docks and got to know the boats and the men.

In the summers, I took what work I could to prove myself. I learned how to tie leaders and how to make lobster traps. And when I turned sixteen, against my mother's objections and the objections of my teachers, I left school. Two of my teachers even came to the house to try to talk to my mother and me. They said I was making a huge mistake. That in two years if I kept studying that lots of colleges would be interested in me. My mother agreed with them but I said, we don't have any money. Keep your grades up, Anthony, they said, and the money will be there. They said it like the money would just appear out of nowhere. I told them I needed to fish. But that I would work on my G.E.D. when I was home and we would see what happened. Berta didn't talk to me for a few days and I took a job on a boat that jigged for cod. She acted as if by leaving school a part of me had died, which I suppose now it had.

Six months later I would join a swordboat. It was as close to my father as I would ever come.

During the season, I worked as often as I could. I crewed on the *Lorrie Anne*, a good boat for the fleet. I worked like a dog when at sea and at home I had a little change in my pocket. I lived with my mother still but Victor had come to a breaking point with his own father and had managed to get his own place, a studio apartment on Main Street. It was above a seasonal clam shack and in the summer the smell of fried food filtered through his windows all day. But he had a good landing on the wooden staircase in the back and on warm days we could sit out there in beach chairs and smoke cigarettes and look across the road to the harbor and the men working on the wharves. Victor got a job at O'Brien's Funeral Home, which was an odd job until you realized that the only things around here were death and fishing. Victor had never wanted to fish and I figured he was afraid of the sea and I never said anything about it. Many men were afraid of the sea and there was much to be afraid of. Victor was short and stocky, built like a fire hydrant. He had a new mustache in those days that he was always combing. I gave him a hard time about it but he said I was just jealous because I couldn't grow one. Which was true. Even today, my face is almost as smooth as a baby's.

When I wasn't on the North Atlantic, we'd hang out at Victor's apartment or out on the jetty where we could watch the boat traffic coming through the breakwater. If we were lucky one of the older fishermen would buy us some beer to drink. Sometimes we'd go to the mall in Westerly and get something to eat and just walk around. Once in a while, on warm days in the fall and the spring, we'd drive to Providence and sit on the benches on Thayer Street and watch the college girls walk by in their new clothes. They never so much as gave us the time of day, two olive-skinned boys in hooded sweatshirts. We loved to look at them; how pretty they were with their long hair, but it bothered me they didn't acknowledge our stares. I tried to explain this to Victor but he didn't get it.

"Tony," he said. "What do you care? They're rich girls."

And I knew he was right, they were rich white girls, and we were a couple of Portuguese, but I couldn't get it out of my head.

I also did something when we sat on the bench that I never told anyone about, not even Victor. Sometimes I'd see a particular girl, and it didn't have anything to do with what she looked like. They might be blond or brunette, occasionally really pretty, other times more plain. It was more a way they carried themselves that caused me to pick them out. The way they walked, the way they stood, how they looked all around, all of it suggesting to me a sadness hidden from the rest of the world. I was always attracted to sad girls, even before I met her. And when I picked out this particular girl, in my mind I imagined our whole lives together. And while I pictured different things, one image returned over and over again. It was a bright summer day and this girl was in the small yard in front of our house in Galilee. She wore an old sundress and sandals and she had planted flowers and was on her knees tending to them. Her hair was tied up behind her head but one lone strand swung across her forehead. Her hands were covered with dirt and while she worked she sometimes touched her face and there were smudges of dirt from this on her cheeks. She was completely engaged in what she was doing and had no idea she was being watched. I stood in the road and studied her. Over my shoulder was my oilskin bag and I was weary from three weeks at sea. She wasn't expecting me because there was no way to know precisely when I would be back. I would watch her as long as I could, until that moment when she became aware of my gaze, that moment when she looked up and saw me standing there. Then the smile started in her eyes, and quickly moved down her face to her mouth. It took over all of her. She would rise to her feet and wipe her hands on her old sundress, not caring about the streaks she had left on it. She'd run across the small sandy yard then, through the metal gate and out to the road. I'd wait until she reached me before I let my bag slide off my shoulder and hit the ground. I'd smell like the floor of the fish cannery but she wouldn't care less. She'd leap into my arms and I'd spin her, her legs off the ground, while her kisses rained onto my neck.

Everyone knew that house. Where it sat, on the easternmost tip of Cross Island, you couldn't miss it. Our path to the Grand Banks took us right underneath its turret and all the men used it as a landmark. It meant we were only an hour from home.

I don't believe it ever occurred to me that someone actually lived there. It didn't look like the kind of place where people lived. I had no frame of reference for people living in houses that size. It looked like part of the landscape itself, sitting as it did above the granite cliffs, near where the corner of the island hit the broad Atlantic, leaning out over the water like it was one good storm away from tumbling in.

Then one night on the jetty, Victor brought the house into my life.

This was the summer I turned seventeen and Victor and I spent practically every ounce of free time we had out on the jetty. It was our place. We'd drink beer out of cans and sit under the stars listening to the water and watching the boats slide past us in the dark. We'd smoke cigarettes and talk about girls. Neither of us had any prospects, to tell you the truth. All of the girls we knew were still in high school, which we weren't. Our work took us strictly into the world of men. And we could not go into bars yet. Bars seemed like some kind of nirvana. Even walking past the few dives in town, the door would sometimes be propped open against the summer heat and inside we'd see men we knew leaning against the bar with beers in their hands, arms draped around women who would never have given us the time of day. It appeared to us that you just needed to be old enough, and once you were, you could drink the night away and then know what it was to be between the legs of a beautiful woman.

The night Victor told me about the house was a perfect summer night, clear as can be, and without moon. Above us was the great diffused spray of the Milky Way. Below us the waves lapped against the barnacled rocks of the jetty. The only sound was from the thrum of the diesel engines from passing lobster boats. We had a six-pack of beer. Victor started by saying he had done a wake at the house two nights before. An old woman had lived there alone, he said, had died in the kitchen, and then there was a wake in the house a week later. There was no funeral home on the island so they hired O'Brien's. I thought this was shaping up to be another one of Victor's funny stories about working at the funeral home. Like the one he told about a removal they did from a colonial on the waterfront near Connecticut. Some old fellow had died on the third floor and in this old house the staircases were so narrow there was no way they were going to get the gurney up to get him. So O'Brien had Victor keep the family busy in the kitchen and their eyes away from the window. From upstairs O'Brien just tossed the old man out the window and in the kitchen Victor saw the old man go by and he said he expected to hear a thud when he hit but that he was as quiet as falling leaves. The family never knew.

O'Brien and Victor scooped the body off the lawn and into the hearse.

But this story was different. At the wake, Victor's only job was to stand in this library room in the mansion and look official in his suit. O'Brien always gave him exact orders. How to stand with your arms at your side, look straight ahead and don't smile. If someone asks you a question, then bend forward to listen. It was all about appearances and Victor was pretty good at it, I guess. At any rate, at the wake all the people were in another room on the second floor of the house. This was where the food was and in the library where Victor was stationed nothing was going on. Occasionally someone or other would drift into the room and look at the leather-bound books on the wall, or sit in the big chairs and talk in hushed whispers, hiding their words from Victor who would pretend not to listen. And then, for a while, Victor was all alone. He could hear voices from the other room and once O'Brien poked his head in but that was it. So he did one of those impulsive things that people will do when left alone in someone else's house. He lifted the corner of the Persian rug that covered most of the parquet floor. He told me he didn't know exactly why he did it; he thought that perhaps he wanted to see if the wood was a different color as a result of being protected by the rug. Regardless, what he saw when he lifted the rug was dust mostly, but then some five or six feet in, was an envelope that appeared to be overflowing with green bills.

Victor dropped the rug. He looked around and waited for someone to come back into the room. A full ten minutes passed and then the door opened and an elderly couple came in and sat down in the big chairs in front of the fireplace. They made themselves comfortable and Victor gave up hope of being able to lift the rug again.

When Victor told me this, I stopped him. "Tell me about it again," I said.

"Tell you what," Victor said.

"The whole thing," I said, and Victor sighed for I was always making him say things twice. But he was a good sport and started from the beginning and when he reached the part about the money, I said, "You sure it was money."

"Of course, I'm sure. It was money. Tons of it."

"Why didn't you grab it?"

"Because I thought someone was going to come in."

"And did someone?"

"Well, that couple. Then O'Brien. He was just talking about how fucking rich these people were. Over and over."

I said, "I think I would've grabbed it." Though the truth was I didn't know if this was true or not. Chances are I would have done exactly what Victor did.

"I should've," Victor said, and then he told me that the house was empty now, but that all the things were still inside, which meant that the money was there, under the rug. I asked him how he knew this and he said he heard some of the caterers talking and they said it would be six months before the place was cleaned out. We talked about how the woman had lived alone and had no family. How there was no one for that money to go to. And once we reached this point in the conversation, I think we both knew what we were going to do. We had always been good kids and had opportunities to not be and had not taken them. But it was the summer and we were best friends and sometimes when you're young like that you'll do things together that you won't do by yourself. Victor said the house would be open.

"How do you know that?" I asked.

He shrugged. "It's on the island. It's only rich people. Why would they lock it?"

"That makes sense," I said, and we were walking down the road now, down the road toward doing this thing, in our minds anyway. We began to joke about what we would do with all that money, and talking about how much there actually was. The more we talked about it, the more money there was. Enough money to pay for four years of college. Plus, anything else we wanted to do. We joked about how I would go to college and Victor could come live with me. Then after I would be a lawyer or something and we could share a big house together. Have lots of girls. It seemed so easy. We would ride my skiff out to the island at night and sneak into the house. Find the money. And I wasn't only thinking of myself. I thought too of my mother, of Berta, who cooked in a hot kitchen all day and who, at night, moaned in bed because her back hurt so bad. And I think it probably hurt even more than she let on, for the last thing she wanted was for me to worry about her. Which meant that her moaning was involuntary and that she could not do a damn thing about it. I didn't know how I would tell her I got all this money. But I figured I'd worry about that later. The important thing was what it could do for us. If it could change our lives. If it could take us away from the narrow pathways we had always walked on to something different. We were young and when you are young you think there are shortcuts out there that you only need to find. Shortcuts that older people have kept from us. Both Victor and I believed that this might be one of those. And that it could alter our lives. As it turned out, it could. Just not in the way we had imagined.

Victor and I left the following night under clear skies. The moon had appeared as only a sliver above the harbor and the breeze was light. We were in my fourteen-foot skiff, the one that had been my father's, and the most important thing was the breeze. We were going through open water and anything more than a light chop could be trouble.

I steered the skiff through the rows of fishing boats docked in the inner harbor. Under the lamplights on the wharf we saw men on the decks of boats readying themselves to go out the next morning. Some of them looked up at us as we went by and when they did they waved or nodded at us in the dark.

We left the moorings behind us and the water opened up and I pulled down on the throttle and picked up speed. I followed the buoys toward the mouth. There were other skiffs and men pulling pots in the moonlight. A large trawler returning from Georges Bank came within thirty feet of us and we saw the shadows of men leaning against the railing. I didn't recognize the boat or the men on it but I had been to sea enough times to know what they were thinking. In their minds they were already on land. The catch had been unloaded and the holds scrubbed.

They were sitting in the bar, the open ocean growing more distant with each draft.

We passed the lighthouse at Point Judith and then the breakwater. Behind us the lights of the village shrank to pinpricks. We were in the sound now. This was water I had known my whole life. I knew where all the shoals and shallows were and I kept us away from them. To our right the dark humpback of land stretched toward Connecticut. To our left was Narragansett Bay and we could see the lights of freighters at the edge of the sky. There was the gentle breeze that blew my hair back and if it was not for what we were about to do, I would have relaxed into the ride. I would have enjoyed myself.

Even though the chop was light the hull of the small skiff still smacked against the water and we did not try to talk. We stood side by side, and in front of us the island began to take shape in the dark.

Soon we were close enough that we could make out the high dark bluffs. I turned the skiff to starboard, and we began to trace the western side of the island. The harbor and the main village were on the eastern side and there were no lights here. When we got closer, the ocean was shallow and I throttled down as we rode in the lee of the bluffs and we could hear each other clearly now.

"This is fucking crazy," Victor said.

"I know."

"We don't have to do this, Tony," he said. Victor was the only one who called me Tony. I preferred Anthony but it was okay with me if Victor called me Tony.

"Let's just find the cove," I said. "Then we can bail if we want."

I agreed though I had already made up my mind that I was

going to go through with it. I kept thinking about all the money for college, and about my father. I pictured myself walking with those college girls in Providence. What my father would think if he saw me.

I studied the island to my left. I had only been on it a few times, and not since I was little. We always thought of it as a place for tourists. A lot of the girls we grew up with worked there in the summers. They were chambermaids at the inns. I knew a few guys who rode over to work construction. There were some farms and I had heard about work picking fruit but I didn't know anyone who had done that.

I peered through the darkness and now I saw the first lights from the houses high above the cliffs. The shoreline flattened a little bit here and I could see what looked like a beach. In the distance I heard voices and the steady bark of a dog.

We made our way around the western coast of the small island. There were no other boats and in front of us the star-light shimmered a road through the ocean.

"Over there," Victor said, pointing ahead. I saw where the island started to bend inward. "That's the cove."

"You sure?"

"Positive," he said.

I brought the boat in slowly. It was a small cove but the beach looked sandy. I steered toward it and when we started to bottom out I cut the engine. I climbed over the bow and stood in the surf in my boots and the water lapped against the hull of the skiff. I took the rope and pulled the boat closer and when it stopped moving, Victor clambered over the stern. We were on the island.

I looked around. My eyes adjusted to the greater darkness that was the land at night. The cove in front of us was narrow and defined by rock outcroppings. Above there were small scrub trees that grew out of the cliff face and leaned over us.

I said, "Where's the house?"

Victor pointed to the right. "Up there. Through the trees."

"How do we get there?"

"Ahead," he said. "See? There's a path. It runs up that cliff and kicks out behind the house."

I saw where he pointed. A break between trees. I took a deep breath. "All right," I said.

"Tony?"

"I know, Vic," I said.

"There's not going to be anyone up there."

"We should go," I said.

"Okay," said Victor, and we left the boat and moved toward the trees.

We found the path and it was a well-worn trail of packed dirt. On either side of us were small trees and dense undergrowth. The trail itself was narrow. We walked slowly. We didn't want to trip over something we couldn't see. My eyes grew more accustomed to the dark and we went a little quicker. Now and again we stopped and stood next to each other breathing heavily and we listened but there was only the sound of our breathing and the light surf against the beach below.

"Not much farther," Victor said.

Soon the trees on our right thinned and then they fell away completely. I could see the end of the cove and the ocean, though I couldn't see the boat since it was right underneath us. We followed several switchbacks and I got a sense of altitude. I looked to my right and saw the light at Montauk. It was a familiar sight and it comforted me to see it. The land started to level and in front of us the path widened. The trees on either side of us were larger now that we were away from the cliff but in the dark we could not tell what kind they were. The path was wide enough for several people to walk side by side now. In front of us I saw the stars in the sky and when we walked through a small stand of trees we found ourselves on a large lawn and then there was the house, several hundred yards away.

We stopped. The house was massive, huge and black against the expanse of sky. We were looking at the back of it. I sank to one knee, and Victor followed. I felt the grass wet on my jeans.

"The front door is on the other side," Victor whispered.

"No lights on," I whispered back.

Three chimneys rose off the roof and high into the sky. The large turret, the one I had seen from sea, was on the ocean side. We kneeled there for what seemed like a long time. Finally I said, "Stay here."

"You sure?" Victor said, and he sounded relieved. The truth was that I wasn't sure. I only thought it might be easier if I did this alone.

"Yeah," I said. "Look for cars or lights. If anything happens, meet me at the boat."

I didn't say anything else after that. I remembered that when we were younger we used to jump off the bridge into the tidal river that ran near our neighborhood. We were both scared to jump but we would never admit it. I could only jump if I didn't spend time thinking about how far down it was. I needed to hurl myself off as soon as I got up on the trestle. I needed to feel my body in the air and then the water when I hit. That was the way I felt looking at the house. That I couldn't think about it too much. Just get up and run. Do this thing.

I stood and ran across the lawn in a half crouch and I didn't stop until I reached the back of the house. I was in its shadow and I looked back to where Victor was but I could not see him. I leaned against the wall and its shingles felt as cold as water against my bare arms. My breath was coming hard and fast and

I told myself to calm down. I looked up. The roofline looked like it was miles away.

Leaning against the wall, I noticed that there were doors on this side of the house. Places where the wall recessed into itself. Three of them that I could see. I wished Victor was here now, because it might be a good idea to try one of them. But Victor had only described reaching the library from the front door. The last thing I needed was to get lost in a dark house. I started to work my way toward the front.

At the corner of the building I stopped. In front of me was a circular driveway and a road that led to it. The road curved away through the trees. To my right I saw the ocean again and it was a remarkable view even in the thin light. Only the rich had views like this. The land opened up along a cliff walk and then curled back away toward the other side of the island. The sliver of a moon sitting above it all. There were no cars in the driveway. Victor must have been right. No one was here.

I rounded the corner and in front of me was a stone porch. I stayed as close to the building as I could until I reached it. I stepped onto the porch and now I stood in front of the door and I had never seen a door quite like it. Made of heavy dark wood, someone had carved two trees on either side of a leaded-glass window. The trees came together as one above the window, their branches meshing together at their skinniest points. The window was high enough that despite being six-foot-two I had to get on my tiptoes to see through it.

I saw the bottom of a staircase and not much else. I took the large brass doorknob into my hand and I just held it, then I thought again of jumping off the bridge into the tidal river. Don't think too much, Anthony, I told myself. I turned it and it gave way and the heavy door moved inward. The hinges creaked slightly. When it was open just enough for me to slip through, I did, and I found myself in a large hallway. Suddenly, everything felt like a dream. Somewhere came the beating tick tick tick of a clock and I felt things slowing down. I was aware of my every movement, the twitch of a muscle, the blink of an eye.

I left the door behind me partially open. In front of me and directly to the right was a staircase, wide and with a thick wooden railing on the left side of it. Halfway up, it came to a landing and then the stairs curved away to the right. I stepped forward and on my left was a large room that appeared to be completely empty. It had floor-to-ceiling windows and moonlight passed through them and made rectangles on the floor.

I went to the stairs and began to climb. I tested each step for creaks. There was a carpet that split the dark wood of each step and I made sure I stayed on it. I had my left hand on the railing and I propelled myself forward.

I reached the landing and then up the final stairs and I stood in a large foyer. It was darker up here and for a moment I didn't move. In front of me were wide openings—bigger than doorways—that led to other rooms. Victor had said the library was on the right but as it turned out there were two openings on the right. I figured he must have meant the far right and this was the one I took.

It was a large room and despite the darkness I could see the books on the wall stacked neatly in ceiling-high shelves. I had guessed right. I went to my knees and began to crawl forward. I felt around with my arms for the carpet and I did not see the small table until it was too late. I bumped it with my shoulder and I heard something tottering. I reached out with my hands, hoping to catch whatever it was but I missed it and a large table lamp crashed to the ground.

I froze where I was. I did not move. I waited for a minute and then another and I heard nothing except my own labored breath. I went forward again, like a blind man, my hands in front of me. I felt the rough wool of the carpet and with my hands I traced the edge of it to the far right corner. I was as careful as I could be and my only hope was that there was not another table or another lamp to knock over.

When I reached the corner, I half stood and I began to roll the carpet back as far as I dared. Then I returned to my knees and I began to scour the floor with my hands, moving my palms in circles across the wood like I was waxing it. The fingers on my left hand touched it first. I grabbed it and I knew right away that it was what we had come for. I picked it up and it was thick in my hand. I brought the envelope to my face and I thumbed the bills inside it. I stood now and since it was too big for my pocket, I stuffed it into the front of my jeans, against my bare skin.

I left the room the same way I had come in. I wanted to run. But I knew this was a bad idea. I needed to keep my head. I needed to get back down the stairs and out in the night where I belonged.

I crossed the foyer and began down the stairs. One at a time. I reached the landing. The longest part of the stairs were in front of me. It was not far now but it seemed like a long way away. I was looking to see if I could see the front door from here, the door I had left ajar, and if any of the night had spilled into the house. I went to take another step and as I did, the foyer behind me, where I had just left, filled with light.

My heart rose in my chest. I felt it flutter like a bird. I had been afraid many times but not like this. I was no longer alone and I knew I should run. For some reason I could not move. I leaned into the shadows and I looked back toward the light.

And what I saw was a girl, a girl surrounded by golden light and wearing a white nightgown. Through her gown I could see the outline of her legs. I could not see her eyes and I could not tell the color of her hair. But the part of her face that I could see, draped in shadow, was more beautiful than any face I had ever seen. Her high cheekbones and her full lips and her strong nose. Part of me understood that I should not be considering any of this, that I should just run, but something kept me completely still. I had one job in that moment, and that was to move my feet, to get back to the trail, to Victor, and then to the skiff. Back to Galilee. But I couldn't stop staring at her. I was transfixed. And then she spoke.

She said, "Who are you?"

"I won't hurt you," I managed to say and then I repeated it. "I won't hurt you."

"Why are you here?" she asked.

"A mistake," I said, and I wanted for some reason to explain it all to her but I knew this made no sense. I wanted to tell her how we thought the house was empty and that the money didn't belong to anyone. That maybe it would help me get to college. I wanted to say something about how beautiful she was in the golden light and I wanted to ask her the color of her eyes. But I knew that I couldn't do any of these things.

"I have to go," I whispered, as if this was the reasonable thing to do now. I turned away and I began to bound down the steps.

I took them two at a time and in the dark I did not see the man until he was right in front of me. He came up the stairs as fast as I went down.

"Get over here," he said, and I tried to sidestep him. He

was bigger than I was and when he wrapped his arms around me I felt his breath hot against my face. I shook him off and he kept coming. For a moment he was gone and then I felt him again, and he was on top of me, on my shoulders, and he was trying to take me down. He was a very strong man and the weight of him drove me into the railing. I flailed at him with my arms and I think I cried out. I smacked at his hands and I wanted nothing more than to be free of him and then, all of a sudden, I was. He had gone over the railing and landed on the floor below. I heard him hit. It took a minute for it to register and I stood there dumbly looking into the dark.

I heard the girl now and when I looked up she was coming down the stairs toward me, quickly, two steps at a time. "Daddy," she called, saying it over and over, and something inside me broke and I started to run. I ran as fast as I could. I flew down that staircase, and I raced for the open door and through it and I was out on the porch and then onto the lawn.

I tore around the corner of the house and sprinted across the dewy grass and when I reached Victor I said, "Come on," and I kept running. His face looked empty, his jaw slack, brown eyes just staring at me. I ran so fast I almost went off the path and into the undergrowth that was the top of the cliff. I heard Victor panting behind me and when we reached the cove I said, "Get in" and Victor said, "Oh, Jesus," but I barely heard that.

We shoved off from the beach and when the skiff was in water deep enough, I started the engine and it went on the first try. I pulled down on the throttle and turned the boat toward open water.

We rode straight out to sea and we did not talk. I pushed the skiff as hard as I could and when the island was no longer visible in the dark behind us, I cut the engine. The mainland was to our right now and we could see the dim lights from the villages of Galilee and Jerusalem. The boat rocked slightly in the wake. I turned to Victor and before I could say anything I saw in his eyes the fear and I knew it mirrored my own. I tried to tell him what happened but speaking was difficult and my words kept coming out mangled. Finally, I said, "There was a man."

"Where?"

"On the stairs."

"Shit," said Victor. "They said it was going to be empty."

"And there was a girl."

"What? Where?"

"A beautiful girl," I said. "I mean crazy beautiful."

"Tony, I don't get it."

I ran my hand through my hair and I looked toward the point and to where the lighthouse beam cut a swath across the water. I told Victor everything at once. I told him about going into the house. About climbing the stairs. Knocking over the lamp and then finding the money. I told him how the light went on at the top of the stairs behind me and how I turned to see the girl standing there. How I could see all of her when the light passed through her gown. I told him how lovely she was. I tried to capture her shadow-draped face for Victor but words alone could never do her justice. There was nothing to do but to stare, I said, and this was why I did not see the man until he was on me.

"But she didn't see you?" Victor asked.

"No," I said. "No, I don't think so. She couldn't have. It was too dark. I was in the shadows. Listen, light me a cigarette, will you? My hands are shaking too much."

Victor lighted a cigarette and then lit another one off of it. He handed one to me and I drew on it and underneath the boat I felt the swell of the ocean, where it lifted us up and let us back down again. I looked deep into the distance, into the black horizon, and I saw where the sea became sky and where the stars touched the earth.

"But the man," I said.

"What?" said Victor and in his voice I heard the alarm.

I sighed. "He fell. Fell a long way, I think. He tried to tackle me on the stairs. I shook him off. At least I think I did. He was gone. Over the railing."

"Jesus, Tony," Victor said. "How far?"

"A long way," I said. "I heard him hit. On the wood floor. I heard him hit on the wood floor."

"He's okay, though, right? He's okay?"

I shook my head. "Shit, I don't know. It was a long way."

"It was an accident," Victor said hopefully.

"I don't know," I said.

"It was an accident," Victor said again, and this time I didn't feel like consoling him. I was the one who had gone in the house, the one who had been there.

I said, "I don't know, Vic. We were robbing the fucking house."

did all the time and so

We rode the skiff toward the mainland and approached Galilee from the west, as if we had been fishing the shoals down coast. It was something we often did in the summer and maybe on any other night we would have looked only like two fishing buddies, throwing a line to pass the time.

The harbor was quiet when we crossed the breakwater. One trawler was heading out but it was late and there was little other activity.

I tied up the skiff and we walked along the darkened wharves and then past the cannery without speaking. In an alley between warehouses a drunk on his knees retched and when we went by he looked up at us. At Main Street we stopped for a moment before we split up. I thought there was something I needed to say but I did not know what. I knew I didn't have to mention the money because neither of us wanted to think about that now. I would put it away and try to forget about it.

"Call me tomorrow," I said.

"Sure," said Victor, and he held his hand out, palm up, and I smacked mine, knuckles down, against it. It was something we did all the time then, and it felt silly this night, it felt forced, as if nothing had happened in the last couple of hours. Like it was any other night when we didn't have to work.

I watched Victor walk toward the studio apartment he rented above the restaurant. I didn't want to go home just yet so I lighted a cigarette and stood with the yellow from the street-light above me spreading across the black pavement at my feet. Now that I was alone, I was suddenly exhausted. I felt the tired in my arms and in my legs. I wanted my bed but I needed time to think. I walked the deserted streets for a half hour, thinking on the night. Finally, I turned down my narrow street, the small bungalows all in a row; mine the only one showing any light. My mother must have fallen asleep in front of the television.

Sure enough, when I opened the door she was in the re-clining chair, a late-night show on in front of her. A blanket covered her stout legs and looking at her wide, pleasant face, her closed eyes, a strong feeling of love washed over me.

"Berta," I whispered.

She slowly opened her eyes. She gave me a sleepy smile and she stretched. "Anthony, *bonito*," she said, and then she frowned. "You were out late."

"Fishing with Victor."

"Fishing," she said. "Always fishing."

"It's something to do," I said.

"Help me up," she said.

I took her hands in mine and they were rough like a fish-erman's hands and this always surprised me. I knew it was from all the work in the kitchens but I expected them to be smooth. I always thought a mother's hands should be smooth. I pulled her to her feet. When she stood her head only came to my rib cage and I hugged her.

"Work comes early tomorrow," she said.

"I wish you didn't have to go," I said, and I remembered the money in my pocket.

"No rest for the wicked," she said, and she smiled and leaned up and kissed me.

"Good night, Mama," I said.

In my bedroom I opened the window and I looked out to the other houses and the small sandy yards with their chain-link fences. I dangled one leg out in the air and I lighted a cigarette. Berta hated when I did this but she had stopped saying anything to me a while ago. The wind had picked up since we had left the water and I listened to it move through the stubby trees.

I looked back into the room and to the bureau where I had put the money when I came upstairs. When I took it out from under my shirt, there it was, all those bills. I had not intended to count it. But when I saw them spilling out, I couldn't help it. I took them out onto the bed and they were all thousand-dollar bills and I had never seen a thousand-dollar bill before. I picked one of them up and on front was Grover Cleveland. Fat with a thick mustache. I laid them out on the bed, one next to the other. There were sixteen of them. Sixteen thousand dollars. More than Berta made in a year. Enough for college, I thought, though I did not know that.

I tucked the bills in among my socks. Now my thoughts turned to the stairs inside that great house. If only I had not melted into the wall. If only I had been able to stop staring at the girl. If only I had run when the light came on. Then I would have made it outside before her father reached me. He wouldn't have been able to tackle me. I wouldn't have ridden him into the railing and he wouldn't have fallen. And I wouldn't have heard him hit below. There was nothing terribly human about it, the sound of him. It was like a sack of flour had dropped to the floor.

I woke to rain, heavy, driving rain, coming down so hard that to look out the window was like looking into the back side of a waterfall. I was just staring at it blankly, and I had this strange feeling, like I had been awake for a while and I didn't know it. The phone was ringing. It had been ringing for a long time, I realized. The incessant peal of it. When I finally trotted downstairs in my underwear to answer it, Victor told me that the man had died. It was all over the papers and on the radio and the television. His name was Jacob Forbes, Victor said. His daughter, the newspaper said, was named Hannah Forbes and she was the lone witness to the robbery. They were from Boston. The house had belonged to his late mother. Victor went on about all the details. Police searching for two men in a boat and all that. Nothing appeared to be missing, etc. And to be honest with you, I stopped listening to him when I heard her name. Hannah Forbes. I said it a few times over and over in my mind. There is something that happens when something that had previously been unnamed becomes named. It becomes more important somehow. Or maybe just clearer. Either way, hearing her name did something to me. As Victor read the article to me, I pictured the girl sitting in some cold police station, in a metal chair next to a metal desk. Perhaps she had a blanket slung over her shoulders since she had not had time to change yet. Her long hair hung down over the bars of the chair. She was crying. A police officer consoled her, and I wondered if it broke his heart to watch a pretty girl cry.

I met Victor for lunch at his apartment and he chain-smoked and paced back and forth and said we should turn ourselves in. He showed me a copy of the *Journal* with its front-page picture of the mansion in daytime, when it was even more impressive, rising up against an uneven sky.

I said, "We can't turn ourselves in."

"What else we going to do, Tony?"

"Listen, I was the one who went in there. Not you. I'm the one who'd go to prison. That's not going to happen."

"How many people, Tony, saw us leave the harbor last night?"

"Lots of people left the harbor," I said. "And not only our harbor. They got to be looking at everything from Fire Island to the Vineyard. We do what we normally do and we have nothing to worry about."

This seemed to relax him a little bit and when I left, he promised to call me if he heard anything else.

That afternoon the rain clouds moved off the coast and the sun that burned through was summer hot and as I walked to my skiff the puddles on the pavement steamed from its heat. I walked across the wharves and past men baiting lobster traps with baby skate and stacking them onto the flatbed of an old rustbucket. Other men stood in huddled groups smoking and I knew some of them and they'd call "Hey, Anthony," to me or I'd shout out to them. When I reached my skiff, I spent a few minutes just peering down into the black water, to where oil had collected around the pilings and shone a rainbow in the sunlight. Maybe it had something to do with the rainbow, this piece of beauty among the filthy oil, but standing there, I started to cry. I looked around to make sure no one saw me. And I cried good and hard, harder than I had since my father died. I saw men going out on their boats and I knew that there was one less man in the world and it was because of me. That I had killed somebody. It didn't matter that it was an accident. It didn't matter that the last thing I wanted to do was to kill a man. It had happened and it was my fault.

After a while, the tears slowed and I got them under control. I rubbed at my eyes. Then I climbed in my skiff and I maneuvered my way through the fishing boats and followed the buoys to the mouth of the harbor.

The bank of clouds loomed over the horizon to the south now but here it was so clear I could see the bluffs of Cross Island. I was suddenly tempted to follow our path from the night before, to ride under the turret of the house and see what I could see. But instead I turned down coast and I spent the rest of that summer day fishing the shoals. It was a half-hearted effort and I didn't even have live bait. But I found that the rhythmic tossing of the line over and over, and the gentle rocking of the small craft, soothed me. I did not cry again that day. You would think out there alone like that my mind would race, that I would have become overwhelmed with fear. But I gave in to the simple pleasure of casting the surf rod, watching the speckled lure tumble through the air before diving under the waves near the rocky shore. The reeling in when it danced like a mouse across the surface of the water. I would've probably stayed out until late if it were not for the fact that I had forgotten to eat. The hunger came on like a rush and I put my gear away and turned back toward town.

By the time I reached my street, I was so hungry that the only thing on my mind was what Berta might have on the stove. She usually cooked for two and left mine for me to reheat. She made a great peppery kale soup with lots of sausage. And sometimes they cleaned out the walk-in at the college and she brought home a chicken or some beef. I was so engrossed with the possibilities, that I almost didn't notice the red-and-white sheriff's car parked right in front of our house until I stood right next to it.

For a moment I considered just taking off. But then I remembered that there was nothing to tie us to the house and the island. Only people who had seen us leave the harbor. Unless the girl had actually gotten a good look at me, but I didn't think that was possible. Or if Victor had already caved, though I didn't think he would do that. Not without talking to me about it first.

Sheriff Riker was a tall, hawk-nosed man, close to sixty it looked liked, with slicked-back hair and the leathery skin of someone who spent far too much time in the sun. My first thought was that his was not an unfriendly face. He wasn't in uniform but wore a golf shirt and khakis, boat shoes. He was on my mother's couch and drinking my mother's coffee and I had no idea how long he had been there.

"Here he is," Berta said, when I came in the door.

"You must be Anthony," the sheriff said, and he introduced himself and took my hand and we all sat down.

"I don't know if you heard about what happened on the island last night," the sheriff began.

I shook my head.

"It's been on the news," he continued. "Anyway. There was a robbery. Well, attempted robbery at a mansion on the eastern side of the island. Nothing was missing. But there was a fight and a man was killed. We're trying to find out who was in the house."

I looked right at the sheriff. I was trying not to blink. "What's this have to do with me?"

"Nothing, I'm sure," he said. "It's just that a number of people saw you go out last night."

"I went fishing."

"Who were you with?"

"Victor," I said. "My friend."

"Last name?" the sheriff asked. From the pocket of his pants he took out a small notebook and one of those golf pencils.

"Perez," I said, and he wrote this down and closed the book.

"Where were you going?"

"We went fishing."

"He often fishes at night," Berta offered.

"Where'd you fish?"

"The shoals," I said. "Down coast."

The sheriff nodded. "What were you after?"

"Stripers. They're running a little bit."

"Good eating," the sheriff said.

I shrugged and gave him a smile. "We didn't have any luck."

He said, "You didn't go anywhere near Cross Island?"

"Have you seen my skiff?"

"No," he said.

"It's small. I stay close to shore."

"All right, Anthony," the sheriff said. "You going to be around if I have other questions?"

"Until Monday."

"Where you going then?"

"I crew on the *Lorrie Anne*. The Grand Banks."

"Scalloper?" he asked.

"Swordboat."

"Have a safe trip," he said, and he rose. "Thanks for the coffee, Mrs. Lopes."

My mother nodded and the sheriff left. Through the open door we watched his cruiser start up and then drive off. I wanted to call Victor but I knew I couldn't do that yet. Berta looked up at me. "Anthony," she said, "you didn't have anything to do with this. What the man said."

"No, Mama," I said, and I saw her looking over at the one painting we had in the house. It was a Madonna with child and it was somewhat abstract, the Madonna with a big golden triangle over her head, the dark-skinned baby's face featureless. Berta crossed herself and this bothered me, and I said, "Don't cross yourself, Mama, I didn't do anything."

"Old habits," she said.

We ate dinner together that night, clams from the college that needed to be used that day with tomatoes and chorizo and toast. After, when my mother went upstairs, I tried desperately to get Victor on the phone but all it did was ring and ring. Eventually my nerves got to me and I crept out of the house and made my way through the darkened village to his apartment. His old Chevy sedan was gone and the lights were off upstairs. I decided to wait for him. I sat at the bottom of his staircase and smoked and watched the moon rise above the commercial buildings across the street. When he finally returned, I did not have a cigarette lit and he didn't see me until he was right on top of me. I scared the shit out of him and he jumped. I laughed.

"Asshole," Victor said.

"Sorry, Vic," I said.

As it turned out the sheriff had not been to see him, and Victor freaked when I told him the sheriff had come to my house. I told him the fact that he had not come to find Victor right away was a good sign.

"I was at work," Victor said.

"You think they can't find you at work?"

I told Victor we just had to be ourselves, do what we would normally do, and we had nothing to worry about. "You think so?" Victor said.

"Yeah," I told Victor. "I do."

"Okay, Tony," he said, and we sat in silence after that. We could hear the seagulls near the cannery and the occasional bleat of a boat's horn. The light from the point strafed the sky.

By Monday, Victor still had not been contacted by the sheriff and we figured we were safe. And that morning, before the sun rose, I said good-bye to my mother in the hallway of our small home and I saw in her eyes the sadness I always saw when I went to sea. Before me she had looked at my father this way and he had told me that a woman's sadness was to be welcomed. Many men did not have anyone waiting for them when they went to the Grand Banks.

An hour later we were steaming out of the harbor. It would be weeks before I would see my home again and I stood on the deck and watched the land recede behind me. Carlos and I were on the deck. Big Al and Ronny were below, sleeping off whatever they had done to themselves the night before. Captain Alavares was in the wheelhouse. Carlos, a heavy-browed Portuguese of about forty, was already tying leaders. This was work we shared and he knew I was good for my end so he didn't say anything when I hadn't started yet. There was a bright blue sky and a few high cirrus clouds. The truth was that I wanted to see the island. I wanted to see the house.

We followed virtually the same path that Victor and I had,

though now we were farther from shore and we were steaming much faster than we had in my skiff. The island came into view and then we were passing it. Carlos paid no attention but I stood against the rail and stared up at it. At its craggy bluffs and uneven coastline. And then at the turret of the great house and, coming around, the house itself. I saw a piece of green lawn in front of it and I was far away but I could have sworn I saw a figure standing on it. Was it the girl? And did she look down and see our boat chugging by and see me standing at the rail looking up at her again?

Past the island all that was in front of us was blue ocean. This was when I needed the work, the busy work that went with the ride out. For without it, I missed the certainty of land too much. You couldn't think about it because if you did it would drive you crazy. You needed to focus on the tasks in front of you, on the cleverness of your fingers.

Among the swordfish fleet, the *Lorrie Anne* was considered a good gig. As a boat it had never had any problems and Captain Alavares had a nose for fish. He didn't tolerate any bullshit, no drinking or drugs, and he hired good people and we made money.

I know that before I came on, some of the other men thought I was a Jonah, someone who was cursed. They never said it to my face, but I saw it in their eyes, and in the way conversation stopped when I came below. This was on account of my father drowning at sea. Though Captain Alavares had known my father, and knew he had been a good and able fisherman. And after a number of trips, Carlos and Ronny, the butcher, and Big Al, the cook, knew me too and I was no longer a greenhorn and we got along just fine.

It took five days to get to the swordfish grounds. Once the

lines were readied, there was nothing to do but wait. During the days we sat in the galley and chain-smoked and watched movies. We watched the same ones over and over. Like *Scarface*, which we all knew by heart. We took turns saying the lines out loud. Sometimes I lay in my bunk and read. The other guys made fun of me for it for they never read books. Big Al fed us twice a day and we looked forward to the meals as much for relief from the boredom as for the sustenance. Big Al was a pretty good cook. And we had all his best meals on the way out, the flank steak and the chicken parmesan and the stuffed had-dock. Once we were working it was all spaghetti and salad. Not that it mattered then for we were working eighteen hour days, and none of us knew whether it was night or day, whether it was raining or clear, let alone what we shoveled into our mouths.

Until then, though, the only other responsibility we had was to take a turn at watch during the night. We divided the night into two-hour shifts and as the youngest, I got the worst time, two to four, smack in the middle and perfectly designed to make sure I could not string together too many consecutive hours of sleep. Our job was to sit in the wheelhouse and moni-tor the instruments. Every half hour we checked the engine room. And we only woke the captain if we saw another ship on the radar, which didn't happen too often. The North Atlantic was pretty much empty on the way out.

Sitting in the captain's chair that first night, with the only light coming from the instruments, looking to the sea of ocean stars above, I could not help but feel suddenly small, and alone, and afraid. The boat moved in a gentle swell and there was nothing but black ocean in all directions. I tried to think of other things, of home, but the fear kept moving through me. I kept seeing the man falling over the railing. And while that night it happened so fast and it was dark and I had sensed him falling, had heard him falling, rather than seeing him, in my mind when I was on watch, I saw it clear as water. His arms and legs outstretched like he was flying. His face down. All of him moving quickly to the hard floor.

I tried to put it out of my head and think of other things. I looked out to the black ocean. It was so endless in the dark. You might think that after what happened to my father, and the age I was when it happened, that I would be scared to death of the open ocean. But I wasn't. To be honest, I was never afraid of dying. I know that sounds crazy, but it's true. I was afraid of being afraid. A few times we had been in weather so bad that the waves were smacking with fury against the windows of the wheelhouse. We sat huddled in the galley smoking and none of us said a word and we did not have to. We knew that all it would take would be one rogue wave and we'd be beam-to, on our side. It had happened to many boats and when it happened there was nothing you could do but hope the ocean picked you up and laid you back down the right way. Otherwise, you were going down. Trapped in a steel cage with men you knew but could not say you loved.

And that's what scared me. Thinking about those moments of complete self-awareness, when we knew the boat was sinking, when we saw it on each other's faces. What would that fear be like? Would it be raw, like a punch to the face? Or would it be more quiet, the kind that would take us to our knees?

I never told anyone this, but that's why I think the dying would be the easy part. Just close your eyes and go to sleep.

And sitting in the captain's chair, staring at the stars, I wondered why we even did it, took the risk we did for this job. Though I knew the answer already. We did it because we were born to it. We did it because it was the only thing we could do. We did it because in the work itself was a simple truth that is so hard to find in this life. We were men killing fish. It was no more complicated than that. And when you think about it in those terms, you understand the freedom that comes from this work. The freedom in knowing where you stand, in seeing your relationship to things.

We reached the Grand Banks without incident and the weather held. Captain Alavares moved us to different patches of ocean, looking for the right temperature to set. In the galley I sat with Carlos and Big Al and we smoked and waited for the word from up top that it was time to go. Unlike when we were steaming, there was no relaxed banter, no movies. We had our boots on and our coveralls. The quiet anticipation of the work to come.

Then in the afternoon Ronny came down the ladder and said that the captain wanted to see me. If the other men were curious they did not say anything, though I could not remember a moment before when he had asked to see me by myself.

I went to the wheelhouse and when I opened the door, Captain Alavares sat with his back to me and when I walked through he swiveled around and faced me.

"Anthony," he said. "Come in."

Through the windows I could see that the weather still held but the ceiling had shrunk and in the distance there were heavy gray clouds. I stood with my hands clasped in front of my waist, and I said, "Skip."

The captain was in his forties and solidly built, with only the slightest hint of a paunch. The first silver was showing on the hair at his temples. Captain Alavares looked at me. "Anthony, is everything all right?"

I nodded, unclear at what he was getting at. "Yeah, sure," I said.

"I got a strange call on the SSB this morning," he said. "Sheriff from Cross Island."

Immediately I thought of Victor, what he might have done. "Okay," I said.

"You in some kind of trouble, Anthony?"

"Nah, Skip. Not that I know of."

The captain looked straight at me and I tried to return his gaze, but instead I looked past him to where the boat cut through the waves. "He wanted to know if you were on board," he said.

"What'd you tell him?" I said.

"That of course you were on board. He wanted to know when we were coming in."

The captain laughed and I felt better when he did. He said, "Not a fisherman, that one. I told him we'd be in when we were done. Couldn't give him an exact date."

"All right," I said.

"Anthony," he said. "You sure everything's okay? You're not in trouble?"

I shook my head. "Something stupid. Something with my skiff. That's all."

Captain Alavares smiled. "Okay," he said. "Thanks, Anthony."

"We going to set tonight, Skip?" I asked.

He swung his chair around and peered at the instruments

in front of him. "Still running a little cold. But let's hope so. It's time."

We fished that night and every night for the next two weeks. It was a great run with calm seas and clear skies. A pale full fisherman's moon hung fat over the ocean. The first sets we pulled were mainly blue dogs, sharks, but after that it was all swords and big-eyed tuna. We worked hard and I gave in to the rhythm of the work, and the hold quickly grew full. Although in those brief moments when we had a lull, or when I found the time to lie in my bunk, I couldn't help but wonder what waited for me back home. Sometimes I looked to the wake that ran like a road through the ocean behind the boat. And it dawned on me that perhaps my life was going to come to an abrupt end after this trip.

But we caught fish after fish and this meant money and all the men were in good spirits. I tried to join them and sometimes I could not help but feel it. Sometimes I even managed to push it all out of my mind. The sheriff, Victor, the great house. All of it.

One bright sunny morning Captain Alavares told us we had done all we could do. He told us we were going home. We all whooped and hollered and stood dog-tired on the deck putting our arms around each other and lighting cigarettes. The captain turned the boat toward land. We were steaming again. Carlos and Big Al and Ronny all disappeared below to sleep. I stood on the deck and watched the sea move under the boat. I watched the birds that followed us, storm petrels mostly, get pushed around by the breeze. And I wondered if the sheriff would greet me at the wharf, or if he would be waiting for me at my house.

As we approached Galilee, I kept my eyes fixed on the small harbor. After we passed the breakwater, I anxiously scanned the wharf for any signs of red-and-white sheriff cars. But I saw none and when we docked we got busy with unloading the catch and cleaning out the holds and washing the decks. I looked over my shoulder the whole time. When we were done we smoked outside the office while our checks were cut and then we split up, Big Al and Ronny to the bar, Carlos home to his wife, and me to Victor's, where I found his apartment open but my friend nowhere to be found.

I returned to my house and there were no police cars here either. I thought that maybe my mind had gotten to me at sea. It was possible, I thought, that Victor had not caved in like I suspected and told everything. Perhaps the sheriff's call to the boat was nothing more than a routine follow-up. Maybe I was going to be okay, after all.

Inside the house I ate some of Berta's soup and I was so exhausted I kissed her good night while the sun was still in the sky. I climbed into my bed and I slept soundly until I smelled bacon frying in the kitchen the next morning.

At noon, I met Victor at the jetty. The sheriff had been to see him, he told me, though over a week ago, and Victor had done his job. He told him we fished the shoals that night and the sheriff didn't ask him anything else. Victor had not heard a word about it since. There was nothing in the papers anymore. I gave Victor half the money and he didn't want it but I made him take it.

"Don't do anything stupid," I said. "Like get a motorcycle."

The summer moved on. Long days after long days. In July I returned to the Grand Banks and it was another great trip, with fine weather and lots of fish. Both coming and going we steamed under the turret of the house and I looked up at the lawn when we went by, but I did not see anybody standing on it.

For a while, even, everything returned to normal. It was almost as if we had never gone into that house. As if we had stayed on the normal pathway of things the whole time.

Though I never stopped thinking about that night. In my bunk on the North Atlantic when the pitch and roll of the ocean denied me sleep, I returned again and again in my mind to the house. And when I studied what happened as best as I could, something curious happened. I stopped dwelling on the man and his fall. On the death that I was responsible for. Rather, I began to think only about the girl on the stairs. Hannah. To the extent that I considered her father trying to tackle me and then falling, I saw it almost as a separate event, as if it happened on another night. I suppose I knew that this was not right. And perhaps if I thought about it more, I might have realized that the ease with which I did it pointed to some larger flaw that rested within myself. Something that may have always been a part of me, but did not reveal itself until all this happened.

And so it was that as I lay looking at the steel bottom of the bunk above me, it was the girl I was haunted by and it was the girl I wanted to haunt me. I dreamed about her. Once she was on the stairs and she screamed and when I said it would be okay I saw her face visibly relax. Another time it was dark and we lay together in a large bed. All I wanted to know was the color of her eyes. I begged her, let me turn on a light. But she shook her head no and kept inviting me to guess. I named every color I could think of, every color I had ever heard of or seen, but none of them were right.

I also began to see her in other places, when I was not sleeping. Times when I began to wonder if I had lost my mind. She would appear suddenly, out of nowhere, like an apparition. Once I saw her in the shiny black eye of a swordfish. The fish was alive. I had just gaffed it and Big Al and I were struggling to get it up on deck. Its eye was as small and dark as a marble, and when it caught my attention, I saw her in its reflective surface, staring back at me, her long hair streaming behind her. I must have completely stopped what I was doing. For in a moment I heard Big Al next to me and then I felt him, a swift punch delivered to my biceps with his free hand.

"Anthony," he said. "What the fuck? Get her up."

From then on I tried my best to keep her at bay. I tried to think of her only in the deep of night when I was sure I was alone. When I could have her to myself. For the most part it worked. And I didn't tell anyone about this, not even Victor.

One August morning I stood in front of the *Lorrie Anne* where it was berthed. Tomorrow we were to head out again. I was waiting on Carlos. A beautiful midsummer day and we were to spend the morning loading the hold with the squid, work I disliked more than all others. While I waited I stood and smoked and watched the boats around me. Small skiffs and dinghies heading out to larger boats. Trawlers being cleaned and loaded up. The day was warm and the sun moved in and out of high clouds. To my left, rising up above all the fishing boats, was the Cross Island ferry. It left every two hours year-round and we never paid it any attention. A sea bus, we used to call it. Though for some reason this time I was looking at its massive hull and I let my gaze drift up its decks. I drew on my cigarette and when my eyes reached the third level, what I saw almost stopped the heart in my chest.

It was her. Hannah Forbes. She was high above me and the sun was directly behind her head. The way the light shone over her made it impossible for me, once again, to make out her features. But a soft breeze blew her hair back and there was something about the way she stood that I knew with absolute certainty that it was her. You know how a parent can always recognize their child from a distance by how they walk? It was something like that, something intuitive, something I couldn't put my finger on. I said her name out loud then, wanting to hear it roll off my tongue. Hannah. I could not see her face clearly. But I could tell by the way it was angled that she was looking above and beyond me, taking in the harbor, the skiffs and the fishing boats in front of her like toys. I dropped my cigarette and broke into a run.

I ran past Carlos on the wharf, and he said to me, "Whoa, Anthony, man, where you going?"

But all I did was nod and keep moving past him. When I reached the road, I turned toward the ferry terminal. I reached the parking lot and the boat was in front of me. It had left its moorings and was backing out and into the harbor. I scanned the top deck. There was a white-haired couple with sweaters tied around their neck. They waved to a young family next to me. But there was no sign of the girl. Though this time I knew I was no longer seeing things.

When I was first here, they did not allow me to have a mirror in my room and they had to bring me to the barber to shave my face and trim my hair. Now I have a metal mirror of my own and I can look at myself anytime I want. It's hard to be a good judge of oneself, but I wonder if she would recognize the boy I once was. I still have curly hair, though there is a little touch of gray at the temple. My face is a little heavier, especially around the jowls, and from the corners of my eyes crow's-feet radiate out toward my hairline. You can also see my age in the corners of my mouth.

I am different in other ways. I read all the time now. I must go through three books a week. I read all kinds of stuff. I think I like true adventure stories the best. People climbing mountains and having to fight their way out of snowstorms. Or sailing around the world. Men who show extraordinary courage with their backs against the wall.

They encourage my reading and they encourage my writing, though they would prefer it if I would write other things. I told Dr. Mitchell that I am of the mind that we all have one story to tell, one important story, and that this is mine.

"How do you know that?" he says. "You have so much living to do, Anthony."

And when he says this, I'll tell you the truth, I think about it. But then I look out my one window to the manicured lawns and the walkways, and if the leaves are off the trees, I can strain my eyes I and make out the blue-green Atlantic between some of the other buildings. Whenever I see that water, it is this I come back to. This story. Hannah.

In the morning I said good-bye to Berta and when she stared up at me I wanted to tell her that she did not need to worry, that I had no intention of going to sea this time, but I knew she couldn't know this. I didn't say anything to Victor either. He would try to talk me out of it. I lied to Captain Alavares in a note and said I was on my way to New Bedford because of a death in the family. I knew Captain Alavares would not believe me and that I was making his life difficult. I also knew that I was probably forfeiting the right to ever be on his boat again, and I did not care about this either.

An hour later I was on the first ferry to leave Galilee for Cross Island. I wore a Red Sox hat pushed low over my forehead and I had my oilskin bag and inside it was everything I normally brought fishing. All that I would need for a month at sea. Warm clothes and rain gear. A jug of water. My bedroll. A surf rod, separated into two pieces. Tackle. A few ham and cheese sandwiches. A carton of cigarettes and a lighter. Yesterday's *Boston Globe*. And I brought two other things I would not have bothered with if I was going to the Grand Banks. Ten one-hundred-dollar bills that I had exchanged for one of the thousands at the bank. And two bottles of Berta's homemade wine.

I had never been on the ferry before. Fishermen didn't belong on ferries. This early in the morning it was mostly filled with trucks bringing produce and other goods to the island. The truck drivers didn't leave their cabs during the crossing. There were a few tourists and I had worried I might see some of the girls I knew from Galilee, girls who worked on the island, but I did not. I climbed to the top deck and sitting on the blue metal benches were a few older couples. The other day, Hannah had stood on this same deck. I went to the railing and looked out over the harbor and the village. Below me ferry workers in their blue shirts and white shorts untied the ship from the moorings. And, slowly, the ferry began to drift away.

The morning was hazy and ocean-cool. When it burned off, it would be a warm one. Around me, the harbor was waking up. All manner of fishermen readied themselves and their boats to go out. Workers arrived at the cannery and the fish stores. Lobstermen unloaded their catch onto the wharf. The air full of brine and fish and diesel fuel.

This village was all I had ever known. That morning, seeing it from the high deck, from a height greater than I had ever seen it before, it was almost as if I was seeing it for the first time. The working wharves and the gray, featureless commercial buildings. The fish markets and the clam shacks. The small houses in the distance, houses like mine, where the men and women who made their living on this little sliver of coast lived. The bulbous steel water towers inland that loomed over everything. Where the town ended, where the sandy highways that led east to the tourist beaches started. And maybe it was because I had made another choice this day, a choice that would once again lead me away from my life, that it looked so small to me. It looked small and it looked sad.

I turned to the front of the ship. The ceiling was starting to lift and the ocean sparkled in the first sunlight. I could see the rocky bluffs of the island, a mass of brown rising out of the water and toward the sky.

I was the first one off the ferry. I walked down the ramp and past two pretty blue-eyed girls holding the rope open for me. I walked through a parking lot and threaded my way through the line of cars and trucks waiting to board the ferry for the return trip to the mainland. On Main Street the sidewalks were clogged with tourists carrying beach stuff and shopping bags. I pulled my hat lower over my face. On my left large Victorian inns built into the hillside leaned out over the road. On their tiered porches, people sat at tables above me and watched the harbor.

The short Main Street followed the curvature of the island and soon I had left the harbor behind and now there were small Cape houses with porches and yards full of gardens and flowers. To my right the road fell sharply away and below there was a long beach that stretched until the island slipped out of view at other bluffs. High cliffs led to where I walked and this was so different from Galilee, where the land bled right into the ocean. I watched the rippling tide moving unevenly across the beach and into the sand, and the people bathing in the morning sun were scattered like bugs, no more than tiny spots of color.

Cars and couples riding bicycles passed me but no one looked at me twice. I left the town behind and the morning sun warmed my face. On either side of me now meadows of heather and clover rose up and away from me. The road moved inland and I could not see the ocean anymore but I could still smell it. Salt spray hung in the air and the big ocean sky was blue and flat.

At the edge of a small brackish pond I stopped and sat on the grass. I removed the bag from my shoulder and I ate one of the sandwiches. I watched the occasional car driving down the island road. Then I smoked and for a while I just looked across at the rolling land. After a time I rose and began to walk again.

The road meandered through a high country of sedge meadows. Low stone walls crisscrossed bright green pasture-land and along the roadside purple loosestrife grew almost to my belt. This was beautiful land and I saw why the tourists all came here. In the distance weathered gray farmhouses sat on the sloping land and in front of some of them, brown horses in small paddocks flicked their tails against flies. The sun beat down and it was hot now. Not as bad as it was on the open sea but I took off my shirt and tied it around my waist.

As I walked the road began to curve back toward the coast-line and coming around a bend I saw the ocean again, to my right and far below, and somewhere down there was the cove that Victor and I had brought our skiff into that night. I was getting close. The house could not be far now.

Another half hour and I found it. I had walked almost the full length of the island. I stood in front of an ornate iron gate cut into a high hedgerow. I couldn't see all of the house, but I could see a slice of roof, two of the three chimneys and part of the turret, which gave it away. There was no mistaking this house. On the other side of the gate, a winding road cut through the trees.

Now that I was here, I had no idea what to do. It was not like I could just open the gate and walk through it and then knock on the door. What would I say? And in the back of my mind it occurred to me that maybe she had seen me better than I thought that night on the stairs, that maybe she would hear my voice and know that it was me, close the door in my face and call the sheriff.

And as I was thinking this, I heard a car slow behind me. When I turned I saw the rack of lights on the roof and I thought, so this is where it ends.

The red-and-white sheriff's car slowed next to me. I saw the cop inside, and to my relief it was not Sheriff Riker, but a man not much older than myself. I nodded at him and he looked me up and down and then he kept driving. My heart beat like a bird. I watched the car disappear around the bend in front of me and that decided things. I started to walk again.

I followed the road until it turned to the left and began to trace the other side of the island. In front of me was a light-house, another marker I knew from sea. It was a brick building turned a deep rust color from a century of exposure. A parking lot in front of it was full of cars. And on the wide-sloping lawn that surrounded it were hundreds of tourists, sitting on blankets, all here for the dramatic view.

I joined them and sat on the lawn. Far below two strong currents came together on the rocks. The waves moved not toward shore but toward each other, meeting some fifty yards from the rocky beach. Where the waters converged cormorants and gulls dove over and over. The fishing must be good here. Where there were birds there were fish. Though to tell you the truth, this was the last thing on my mind. I wanted to blend in, as much as that was possible. Stay off the road. Figure out what to do next.

made camp on a private beach west of the lighthouse. I had
spent most of the afternoon on the lawn and by early evening
I left and found a general store on the road heading in the
other direction from the way I came. It was a small gray clapboard building and it housed a post office. Inside I cracked
one of the hundred-dollar bills and splurged on a nine-dollar
steak from behind the case. It had been a long time since I
had had a steak. I also bought a can of baked beans and then I
returned to the lighthouse. I followed a path through high sea
grasses and down to the beach where families had gathered to
watch the sunset. I walked through them and then rounded the
point and followed the coastline back toward the cliffs and the
great house. I stopped when I found a beach that looked like it
had not been used for a long time. Above me was a house but
there were no pathways or stairs down to the beach. There was
a rock promontory that hung over the beach and this provided
me some shelter. I had good sight lines in either direction.

After the sunset, I gathered driftwood and with the newspaper from my bag as kindling, I started a fire. Fires were no
doubt illegal but I kept it small. The sun-dried driftwood

burned hot and I only needed it to cook the steak.

I pierced the flesh of the meat with a long stick and when the fire had some coals I held the steak over the flames and I let them lick up the sides of it. I cooked it until it was good and charred on the outside. Then I let it cool by sticking the stick into the sand and letting the meat dangle from it. I opened the can of beans and warmed them in the coals. I uncorked a bottle of Berta's wine. I ate the steak right off the stick and I spooned the warm beans out of the can and into my mouth. I wished I had brought salt and pepper but after a long day of walking I can say that that was one of the best steaks I have ever had. I smoked. After a while I stood and stripped off my clothes. I waded into the surf. The water was shallow and sandy-bottomed and warm. I walked until it was thigh high and then I dove. I slid underneath and closed my eyes and when I came up I floated on my back. The salt water rinsed off all the grit of the day. All around me the color was leaving the world and the darkness rolled in.

followed the coastline and stayed as close as I could to the cliff. I had no idea how far it was in this direction. I had finished three-quarters of the bottle of wine and I was not drunk but I was starting to feel it, not foggy exactly, or euphoric, but somewhere in between. I did know that I wanted to come to the house differently. Not from the cove. It had been a couple of months since Victor and I had gone that way and no doubt it would have been fine but I didn't want to chance it.

The sand was hard-packed beneath my boots and I made good time. At one point the cliff face jutted out into the water and I took off my boots and tied the laces together and rolled up my pants and slung the boots around my neck. To my left was the black sound and the light at Montauk. In between I saw the running lights of boats heading to the mainland. Above there was the crooked moon and the first of the stars. On one stretch of beach I heard voices drifting down from one of the houses. A man laughed heartily followed by the lighter laughter of a woman.

I came upon a wooden staircase built into the hillside. There were no lights coming from above and I didn't hear anything. Two weathered rowboats, overturned on the sand, looked like they had lain undisturbed for a long time. I still didn't know how close I was to the cove, but based on how far I had walked from the lighthouse, I figured it was not far. I climbed the stairs.

When I reached the top, a low-slung modern house sat across a lawn from me. Its large shiny glass windows reflected the moonlight. The wide lawn went as far as I could see on either side of it and I moved across it, heading for a stand of pitch pines.

Once under the trees I stopped and caught my breath. In front of me now was a high hedgerow, the end of the property. I went to it and touched it with my left hand. It was dense and nearly impenetrable. I looked both ways down the length of it. To my left it led to the cliff's edge. The other moved toward the front of the house, and, I assumed, the road. I followed it this way.

I had to go only fifty feet before I came to a small white gate cut into the row. The gate was waist high and latched from the other side but I reached over and opened it. I stepped through it and then underneath some small trees and I found myself looking at the great house. I thought maybe it was two or three properties away but I stood now looking at the front of it. It was giant and still in the dark except for one lone light glowing orange in the turret window.

I kept to the shadows. I moved along the border of thin poplars and cedars that separated the lawn from the cliff walk. When I got about thirty feet from the house, I found a spot beneath three slender trees that afforded me a view directly into the turreted room. The leaves of the trees created an umbrella of shadows from the moonlight. I did not think I could be seen from the window. And if anyone came, I could run back the way I had come, or cut through the brush behind me to the cliff walk.

Through the window I saw a paneled ceiling and what looked like the headboard of a very large bed. But I did not see the girl. It was the only room that was lit. For a moment I thought about going around back as it occurred to me that in a house this big there were probably other rooms that had no relation to the front. And it was as I was thinking about this, that I saw her. It was fleeting and quick but there was no doubt. I stood stock-still. I stared at the window. Even if I had wanted to move, I do not think I could have. And in seeing her, I felt something give inside myself, a feeling I can only describe as becoming unhinged, and I did not know whether to yell or weep, whether to run to the front door of the house or to fall on the dewy grass and just lay there.

Come back, I whispered, please come back.

And a moment later, as if answering my plea, she breezed by the window again but did not stop long enough for me to get a good look. Like that, she was gone and then the light extinguished and I was alone in the dark.

For three successive nights I followed my exact path from the beach and stood in that very spot and looked into her window. I never asked myself at the time if this was okay. It was the reason I was on the island. I stood under those trees and I waited for more than a passing glimpse at her and on that third night, my wish was granted.

She opened the window. She opened the window and she placed her elbows on the sill and she looked out and over me to the ocean. I knew people looked to the sea for answers. What was it she wanted to know? The light was once again behind her and I could not tell the color of her hair or her eyes. And to be truthful it was her eyes I wanted to see because it was a woman's eyes I loved the most.

But I was so happy just to watch her face, the high cheek-bones and the full lips, the way the thin moonlight illumined her pale skin.

I shifted my weight from one foot to the other. Otherwise, I did not move. At one point the breeze picked up off the water and she turned her face into it and the wind lifted her hair off her shoulders before settling it back down again. Was it only the truly romantic that fell in love with someone they had never met? For looking at her, I'm not ashamed to say that that was what I felt. Love. Inexpressible but as real as this great house in front of me. And there was also this: I felt present watching her, more present than I had ever felt before. It was like I had just woken up; it was like blood for the first time decided to pulse through my arteries and spill down my veins. I did not care about anything that came before and I did not care about anything that was yet to happen. I only wanted to watch this girl until she closed the window and turned off the light.

Later that night I sat on the rocky beach and I finished the last of the wine. The breeze coming off the sound was cool and I wanted a fire. But I could not have a fire since it might attract attention. Instead I pulled my coat tight around myself and I smoked until I grew tired.

I laid my bedroll out under the shadow of the large rock and climbed onto it and pulled the open sleeping bag on top of me. I looked up at the stars, clusters ancient and endless. I traced Cassiopeia and Andromeda and Pegasus, constellations that for as long as men took to the sea, they have used to find their way home. Home for me had always been Galilee but now it was this camp, this beach, this water rolling in toward my feet. And when I thought this, I also suddenly felt displaced, like I didn't belong anywhere. The truth was, I was not fully of this beach, and I was not fully of Galilee and I was not part of the *Lorrie Anne.* I had left all that behind. Somewhere out on the Grand Banks my old boat was scouring the fishing grounds for swordfish. And I wondered if the men missed me but then I decided that they did not. Someone had taken my place and fishermen only dealt with the living. Berta missed me, I'm sure, and Victor probably did, too, though he would never admit it.

Once, when I was just a small boy, I was out on the skiff with my father. It was a warm summer night and a clear sky. We were fishing, as we often did, and during a break while my father leaned against the gunwale and rolled one of his cigarettes, he looked up at the full moon, and he said, "The moon is jealous of the sun."

He talked like this to me a lot and he usually had a sly twinkle in his eye and I did not think anything of it. "Why?" I asked.

"Because the sun is always full," he said. "Always fat. The moon only gets to be full once a month. The rest of the time it's hungry. And as soon as it gets full, it has to start all over again." He chuckled. "Kind of like the life of a fisherman."

I remember that I looked up at the moon then, pale and yellow against the black. "It doesn't look jealous," I said.

"Trust me, Anthony," he said. "It is. It's envious. It's an envious moon."

And years later, lying on the beach on Cross Island, looking up at the same moon, I thought that my father probably had it wrong. The moon had the stars. The sun had nothing. The sun was all alone. And no one, I decided, should be all alone.

When I finally fell asleep, I dreamed again about the girl. She was on the stairs and then she was in the window. She told me she was afraid and I said that everyone was afraid. I told her that if she gave me a chance, I could help. Then she lay down next to me and she slung her arms lazily over my chest. I felt the beat of her heart against mine.

I woke once during the night. It was not quite dawn and the sky had turned a robin's-egg blue. I relieved myself against the cliff and for a moment I listened to the shrill cries of the morning gulls diving at the water. I returned to my bedroll and this time I slept without dreams. When I opened my eyes the sun had risen and it was warm. I sat up and shook my head and there, some ten feet from me, was the girl. She sat on a driftwood log with long rubbery pieces of brown kelp at her feet.

I looked over at her. Was I still dreaming? Was she real? She certainly looked real. She wore a white T-shirt and faded jeans and had leather sandals on her feet. Her hair was reddish brown. And, as I had hoped, it was her eyes that brought together the promise of her face. They were green, as green as the phosphorescence that floated under the ocean at night. She was slender and lovely and I had never been happier to see someone in my whole life.

She said, "This is private land, you know."

"I didn't know," I said.

"Are you homeless?"

"No," I said. She picked up a stick and twirled it in her hand. I watched it spin. She wasn't looking at me.

"How old are you?" she said.

"Seventeen."

"Why are you sleeping on the beach?"

"I missed my boat," I said.

"Your boat?"

"The *Lorrie Anne*. It's a longliner."

"A longliner?"

"A fishing boat," I said. "Swordfish."

She looked out toward the ocean, as if maybe she could see the boat I was talking about. "How do you miss a boat?"

I shrugged. "They thought I was crewing with someone else. They left me on the island."

"How could they just leave you? I mean, wouldn't they notice you were missing?"

"I work for a couple of different captains," I said. "If I don't show up, they figure I'm with the other one. It happens more than you might think."

She kept twirling on the stick with her narrow fingers and I saw that she was digesting my story. "You really a fisherman?" she asked.

"My whole life," I said.

She stood then. "I don't care if you stay here. But others will. There's been break-ins. You could get in trouble."

I nodded and she turned to leave. She started to walk away from me, down the beach. "Wait," I called, and she stopped. The sun was behind her now and in its morning light she was perfect. "What's your name?" I said, though of course I already knew.

"Hannah."

"Hannah," I repeated, finally getting to say it out loud. "I'm Anthony."

She smiled at me and gave me a small wave. I watched her walk until she followed the curve of the coastline out of sight.

About a year after I came here, I got a letter. It is written on yellow legal paper. It's five pages long. A woman's handwriting, a beautifully flowing script. The kind they don't bother to teach anymore. Over the years the paper has gotten beat up a little bit from being folded and unfolded so many times. It is creased and the edges on a few of the pages are frayed. When I first got it, I read it all the time. I carried it in my pocket wherever I went. Now I read it less frequently, and never all at once. I like to read it in small pieces. I'm not sure why that it is. Maybe it's just part of getting older. That I prefer to see her in fragments so that I can put her together in my own mind and on my own time. An unadulterated view. In this way, the letter becomes almost an aid. A tool. Something that jump-starts my memory.

It begins:

She was incandescent. Is that the word I am looking for? She glowed. From the moment she came into the world. She glowed. At birth her eyes were blue and she had a little cherub of a face. Big wide eyes. Button nose. Rosebud mouth. Flushed, pink baby skin. Her hair was black then, and it had not fallen out yet and grown back reddish. Just a little patch of black hair. She had a small angel's kiss above her nose. She was very calm, very alert. A really good baby. You just wanted to hold her all the time. Even her cries were pretty. Not piercing like some babies. You just wanted to smell her all the time. She smelled like flowers.

There was a painting in our house, on the living room wall. It was nothing special, something done by one of the island artists. It showed the lighthouse in a storm. The sky was dark and the waves crashed against the cliff. When she was a baby, she liked to stare at this picture. Somehow it soothed her. She could be crying her head off and you would carry her in your arms to the painting. We used to call it the "magic painting." Because no matter how fussy she was, when she saw it, she stopped and stared. Her eyes grew wide. She looked at it like she was seeing God.

She had a favorite blanket. It was chocolate brown and the softest thing you ever felt. We wrapped her in it when she was a baby and years later when she went away to school, it was the one thing she made sure to take with her. She didn't need it anymore for warmth, but it reminded her of her childhood. Carefree and without worries. We loved that about her, that she hung on to things. Not material things, like lots of people, but things that had meaning for her. That reminded her of family.

After Hannah found me on the beach, I debated for a long time what to do next. In the end, I decided the only thing to do was to bring her a fish.

I spent that afternoon below the lighthouse where the waters came together. I stood on an ocean-smoothed rock and the barnacles were enough to anchor myself. The waves washed over my boots. The beach was behind me and in front of me hundreds and hundreds of birds swooped in great arcs toward the water.

I threw line after line into the churning surf. For hours I had no luck. I preferred live bait but all I had was lures. But the test was heavy and the day was beautiful and the ocean breeze felt good against my bare skin. Behind me now and again tourists stopped to watch me cast and I was aware of their presence but I ignored them. I worked different sides of any obstacles I saw. Fish like to gather against objects, rocks and debris. I teased the line through the busy current and I jigged it a little bit. Finally, there it was. Quick as a whisper and it was gone. I brought the line in as fast as I could and I tossed out to the same spot and this time I was ready for it. When it hit I pulled sharply back on the rod. It was a fighter, I could tell that. It wanted to dive and

I gave it some line and let it. Run a little, I thought. Run and get tired. I couldn't tell if it was a blue or a striper. I hoped for a striper. Stripers were less oily and were better eaters. I gave it more line and when it had run for a while, I started to slowly bring it in. At one point it jumped and behind me someone clapped. I had an audience. It rose and I got a good look at it. It was a striper, the blue-green scales bright and silvery in the sunlight.

I felt it tiring. I brought it closer and closer. I wished I had a gaff or a net but it did not matter so much. I brought the bass right to the rock where I stood. I could see it under the water now, laboring, and I reached down and picked it up by the mouth. I held it up in the air for the tourists to see. It was a good fish. Thirty inches or so and fat. I waited until the tourists moved on. Then I swung it hard against the rock until I felt it go slack beneath my fingers.

Back at the camp I gutted the fish and then cleaned it in the salt water. I wrapped it in newspaper and then I took a swim and washed the fish off my hands. When I made my way to the house, I went through the cove this time, following her footsteps in the sand from the morning.

It was strange to walk up the same path in the daylight. I looked at the beach, where my skiff had been that night. And on the trail I suddenly remembered the sound of our feet pounding down it in the dark.

When I reached the house, I marched right up to the door. I held the newspaper-wrapped fish under my arm and I knocked like I was anyone else who had come to visit. I knocked several times and there was no answer.

I sat on the edge of the porch and I waited. I smoked a cigarette and for a moment I worried that perhaps she had left the island. She was probably always leaving the island. Like the time I had seen her on the ferry. The fish was next to me and the day was warm. I could not keep it there forever. I looked down the curvy driveway. This was the way she would come and I hoped that when she did that she'd be alone. I hadn't thought of that. What if she was with someone else? After all, I knew nothing about her. Other than how she looked through a window in the dark.

The afternoon got on. I was about to hide around back, just to make sure that when she showed she'd be alone, when she appeared around the bend on a bicycle. The bicycle was old-fashioned-looking and red and on the front it had a basket. She came to a halt in front of me, putting her feet down on either side of it. Her hair was up in a ponytail. Normally I liked it when girls wore their hair down but this afforded me a better look at her face. And for the first time, I noticed her freckles, the lot of them, like tiny brown stars on her cheeks.

She looked at me, and she said, "What are you doing here?"

I held up the newspaper package. "I brought you a fish."

She laughed. "Are you for real?"

"It's payment. For sleeping on your beach."

She pushed a barrette back on her hair with her right hand. She had to lean back to do this and when she stretched I got a sense of the small breasts beneath her T-shirt. "It's not my beach," she said.

I shrugged. "It's a striped bass. A real nice fish."

Her hands came back to her sides and she crossed her arms on her chest, as if aware of where my gaze had been. Her eyes narrowed. She said, "How'd you know where I lived?"

It was a completely reasonable question and I had antici-pated it. I said, "I followed your tracks. From the beach."

She seemed to be thinking this over. "I don't even like fish," she said.

"This is nice fish," I said. "People who don't like fish like it. It's a white fish. Very sweet."

"I don't know how to cook."

"I'll cook it for you," I said.

"I don't even know you," she said.

I smiled. "I'm Anthony Lopes. From Galilee, Rhode Island. I live with my mother and I missed my boat. I'm a nice guy. You can ask anyone."

"Who could I ask?"

"Okay, look," I said. "If you want, I will just cook the fish and then leave. You can eat when I'm gone. I'm telling you, you will like it. Lock me in the kitchen if you want. I don't care. If you ever want me to go, just say so. I'll leave in a second."

Hannah sighed. "This is so weird. Who does this?"

"I'm a full-service fisherman," I said, and this made her smile. It was a natural smile, the kind she couldn't help, and as soon as she did, I saw her look away from me as if this was something she didn't want to give me yet. Though it was okay for I had already seen it and it was not something she could take back.

"You're really going to cook it," she said.

I nodded. "I'm telling you it's nice fish."

She stepped off her bike and said, once again and to no one in particular, "This is so weird." I knew then that I had her. She wheeled the bike past me and onto the porch and rested it against the wall. She opened the wooden door and turned and looked at me.

"Well, come on then," she said, and for the second time in my life I walked into that huge house.

Standing for a moment in the foyer in front of the staircase, different feelings washed over me. The stairs were to my right and I saw the railing, the one that had come into play that night. And in front of me was a long narrow hallway and its polished hardwood floor gleamed as if it had been recently waxed. This was where her father had hit. Where he had died. I must have been staring at it because she pointed at it.

She said, "The kitchen is that way. Down and to the right. I'm going to change."

She left me then, heading up the staircase, and I walked gingerly across that stretch of floor. To my right I passed the large empty ballroom, one of the biggest rooms I have ever seen. It had floor-to-ceiling windows and its floors were parquet. The ceiling was high and in its center was a massive chandelier. Halfway down the hallway there was a wooden side table against the right wall. Above it were black-and-white photos. I stopped. In the pictures there was a man who must have been her father. He was tall and wide-shouldered, and a full head of hair swept back from his forehead. A big handsome face. A large man, the same man who tackled me on the stairs. In one picture he was standing on a sailboat, maybe a forty-eight footer. The collar on his shirt was up and he wore white pants. In another he held a girl that must have been a young Hannah. Her curly hair the color of the sun. Her legs dangling from out of a small skirt, little buckle shoes on. Her father staring down at her with a look I can only describe as complete adoration. It broke my heart to see that look, that kind of love. Everyone should know that kind of love for as long as they can. I had known it with my own father. And now I had taken it from Hannah.

I found the kitchen where she said I would. It looked more like the kitchens Berta cooked in than one that belonged in somebody's home. It was long and narrow and ran down the eastern side of the house. Everything was stainless steel: the eight-burner stove, the countertops, the refrigerator. The floor was concrete. Glass cabinets held stemware and plates. There were no windows.

I put the newspaper-wrapped fish on the counter and peeled the paper away. It really was a beautiful fish. If I had brought it home to Berta, she would have stretched it into three or four meals. Fried hunks of fillet the first night. Fish stew the next night. And then she'd use the skeleton and the head for a stock for one of her spicy soups we'd eat with bread.

I took the knife from the back of my belt and I removed the head and was about to do the same to the fillets, when I heard her behind me. I turned and she stood there, having changed into a new pair of shorts and a T-shirt. Her legs were deeply tan and shapely where they came out of her shorts, complected differently from her face, which was pale except for the numerous freckles.

"Hello," I said.

"So you really know how to cook?" she asked.

I flipped the fish over. "Yes."

"Where'd you learn?"

"My mother taught me."

"A lot of boys wouldn't admit that."

"I'm not a lot of boys."

"Don't take this the wrong way," she said.

"What?"

"Are you Puerto Rican?"

I laughed. "No, Portuguese."

"I didn't mean it to sound like that."

"We all look alike," I said.

"I didn't mean—"

"I'm messing with you."

"Show me what you're doing," Hannah said.

"Move closer," I said, and she came to the counter and stood next to me. I could smell her soap and it was bright and clean.

"Look," I said. I held my knife down along the body, under the gills. "The fillet is here. You have to make a slice by the tail and then peel it away from the spine. You got to have a sharp knife and work quickly. It can break on you. You want the fillet whole."

"It looks hard."

"Just takes practice."

I held the fish in front of me and made a small incision above the tail of the striper. I worked the flat of the blade in until I reached the spine. I began to scrape and slide, working from feel. I separated it from the length of bone and I pulled the fillet free and showed her.

"See?" I said.

"Cool."

"Wait till you taste it. Fish this fresh is its own thing."

In a pantry off the kitchen I found all that I needed to make Berta's Portuguese sauce. I had never made it myself but I had seen her make it hundreds of times. It was easy. I simmered canned tomatoes with garlic, onions, cloves, and bay leaves. I added some cayenne pepper and the two fish fillets and I let them braise in the liquid. The air filled with the smell of the spice and while it cooked, we leaned against the counter and we talked.

Hannah told me she was seventeen, too, and that she went to boarding school in Connecticut. It was called Miss Watson's and she did not like it much but it was her last year. Next year she would go to college and she thought maybe Smith and she said this like I should know what Smith was but I didn't. I didn't care if she thought I was stupid. There were lots of things I did not know but then again there were lots of things I did. Smith was not one of them. I asked her.

"It's a college," Hannah said. "In Massachusetts. My mother went there. So did my grandmother. I probably will. Go, I mean. Though sometimes I think about going far away. To California or something. Just to piss my mother off."

"I know what that's like," I said.

"To piss your mother off?"

"No," I said. "To do the same thing. My father fished. And his father did. Now I do."

She nodded earnestly. "Oh," she said, "I get it."

We ate outside on the stone front porch and I put the fish on white plates and I covered it with the sauce and when she had taken a bite I looked over at her and I asked if she liked it.

"It's good. Spicy."

"The cayenne. Gives the heat."

"I like it."

"All we need is some wine."

"There's wine here," she said. "Tons of it."

"Yeah?"

"Help yourself. My mother won't notice. It's in the basement. The brown door in the kitchen."

I returned to the house and in the kitchen I found the door and made my way down a rickety staircase into a cavernous cellar. In front of me was more wine than I had ever seen in any store. Rows and rows of it in wooden bins to the ceiling. I reached into the one in front of me and pulled out a bottle. The label was in French but the wine was red and this was what I wanted. In the kitchen I found a corkscrew and brought the bottle outside. Hannah said, "We have glasses, you know."

"Tell me where."

"I'll get them," she said, and she disappeared inside and when she returned with the wineglasses I poured wine into each one.

"Good wine," I said, after sipping from it.

She shrugged. "It all tastes the same to me."

"Crazy how much is down there."

"I only drink it when my friends come from school and want to get drunk."

"I'd drink it all the time," I said. "Wine's good for you."

"My father drank it. My mother just wants vodka."

"Where is your father?"

"He died."

"I'm sorry," I said. "I lost mine, too. When I was little."

"It's hard," she said. "And now my mother wants nothing to do with this place."

"She doesn't mind you being here alone?"

Hannah shrugged. "She'd rather have me in Boston but knows I'd fight it. She wanted someone to come stay with me. She was actually going to hire someone, like a babysitter. I told her I was seventeen. I mean, come on."

I smiled and then I was silent for a moment. I thought of her father. I looked out to the ocean and I searched for something to say. I finally said, "You have a boyfriend at school?"

She laughed. "No."

"What's so funny?"

"My school is all girls."

"I'd be okay with that," I said. "All girls."

"What boy wouldn't?"

"It must be boring for you. All girls."

"There are boys from other schools. They come down on weekends. Or we go up there."

"Do you have a boyfriend from another school?"

"Nosy, nosy," Hannah said.

"Just curious, that's all."

"No," she said. "No boyfriend at another school. Satisfied?"

"Yes," I said.

And we sat in silence after that and presently she rose and took our plates and brought them inside. I looked to where the sun was beginning its descent. The sunset to come was going to be magnificent. The sky was already turning a deep red. To my left was the moon, scarcely more than a tracing at the edge of everything.

I told Hannah what I could about fishing on the North Atlantic and she seemed to want to know it all. I told her about the long steams out to the swordfish grounds and all the busy work that went along with it. I told her about Captain Alavares, and about Big Al and Carlos and Ronny. I told her what it was like when we got weather, and how afraid I was sometimes. How sometimes the fear doubled back on itself and you almost forgot what you were afraid of, that the fear became the thing.

And with each word I uttered, every story I told, I felt her understanding of me grow and grow, and to that point I had never been more honest with anyone in my life. I know that sounds strange given all that I did not tell her that night. All that I left out. But I spoke from my heart and from nowhere else.

Then when I said all I had to say, Hannah said softly, "You can kiss me if you want."

I turned toward her. I slid closer on the stone steps. She laughed at me, and said, "Are you going to?"

"Yes," I said, and I leaned in and she did too and our lips brushed together and then apart.

"Give me a real kiss," she said.

I leaned in again and this time I felt her tongue on my teeth and I opened my mouth and her breath was hot on my face. I had no idea what I was doing but I closed my eyes and we kissed like this for a while. The truth was that all I wanted to do was hold her, to feel her in my arms, and when we came apart, I wrapped my arms around her and I brought her to my chest. Her face pressed into my sternum. She smelled like soap and she was so warm. I lightly played with her hair. And after a few minutes I sensed her tears before I heard them, the sudden heaviness of her breathing against me.

"Hey," I said. "You okay?"

"I'm sorry."

"Don't be."

"I just get sad sometimes."

"I know," I said, and I did, for I got sad sometimes too.

I let her cry then and she cried good and hard against my chest. I stroked her hair but I did not say anything else. In her small fist she balled up part of my T-shirt. I looked over her to the stars and we stayed like this until she fell asleep in my arms.

I wanted to move but I did not want to wake her. She was so peaceful. Her head was heavy against my biceps and when I shifted slightly, she turned her face inward and now I could gaze down onto it. Her soft eyelids and small nose, her pale, freckled skin. Her hair falling over my bare arms. I had never held anyone like this before and I decided then that it did not matter how tired my arm got, or how badly I wanted a cigarette, I was not going to move until she did. She could have stayed there forever for all I cared.

left her at the edge of the stairs and kissed her good-bye and when she had climbed up and out of my sight, I returned to my camp on the beach. I lay on my bedroll and I did not want to sleep. I replayed in my mind the smallest of her gestures—and the larger ones, like the kiss, and I thought I saw in her eyes what had existed in my own for a long time now.

In the morning I returned to the house but she had already left. Another sunny day in a string of sunny days and I lingered around for a while but she didn't return. I spent the afternoon on the beach. I took turns swimming and lying on my bedroll. I hiked to the general store and bought a sandwich for lunch. I lazily threw a line in at one point. It was a beautiful day and I had the sun and the water to swim in. I could fish if I wanted to. There was no work I needed to do. And, I thought, so this is love. For I had the sun and the water and all the time the summer afforded, and I wanted none of them. All I wanted was Hannah.

In the evening I returned to the house and this time she was sitting exactly where we had sat the night before and next to her was a pizza. A large pizza, a pizza for two. Her hands were across her knees and she smiled at me when I came across the lawn.

"I figured you'd still be here," she said.

"Are you trying to get rid of me?"

"Not yet."

"Where you been all day?"

"Work."

I laughed. "You work?"

She looked away, toward the sea. "A condition of my father's while I'm on the island," she said softly.

"Oh," I said. "Where do you work?"

"Benny's Ice Cream," she said. "I'm a scooper."

"I bet you're good at it," I said.

"I'm okay."

"I should've come and visited you. If I'd known."

"We're not allowed to have visitors."

"Then I'd be a customer."

She didn't respond to that. She pulled the cardboard top back on the pizza box. "Onions and mushrooms," she said. "I was going to get pepperoni because that's what guys seem to like but I don't like it too much. Hope it's okay."

"It's great," I said.

We ate the pizza and it was another comfortable evening and the sunset spilled across the sky. I opened another bottle of wine from the basement and we shared it. I could do this every day, I told her. And I could have. Sit on the stone porch and watch the ocean and the day fade from the sky with a beautiful girl. At one point she moved into me and I put my arm around her. I said, "You're not going to fall asleep on me this time?"

"Stay with me," she said.

"When?"

"Tonight."

We shared the high-canopied bed in the turreted room.
The moonlight coming through the windows painted stripes on
the wall. She changed in the darkened room, turning her back
to me and slipping on that cotton nightgown. I watched her
where she stood in the shadows, lifting the shirt over her head,
her hair tumbling down around her bare neck. The whiteness
of her naked back and the curve of her hip and then the gown
covering all of it. When she turned back around she climbed
into the bed, and said, "I won't sleep with you."

"Okay," I said.

I wore only my shorts and she laid her head on my bare
chest and in minutes she was snoring softly. I have never known
anyone who slept so easily. I listened to the rise and fall of her
breath. I held one hand against the small of her back. And when
she rolled away from me, I let her go and the covers fell down
and they only came to her waist. Lying on her side away from
me, I could see now where her neck met her shoulder, where
her shoulder curved toward her arms, where her torso curved
slightly inward before coming back to meet her hip. I saw how
she was made, in other words, how perfect she was. And with
my eyes I traced the shape of her over and over.

Later, when I could not sleep, I rose and walked across the
room to the turret window. I carefully lifted it open and it
creaked a little as I did. I leaned my elbows on the sill, as she
had done the other night. I looked across the yard. I looked
over the cliffs and to the ocean. I stared down at the stand of
pitch pines I had stood under to watch her. And when I did, I
realized they were not as dark as I had thought. I could make
out the individual trunks. They were surrounded by deep shadows, but I saw that if someone were standing out there now, I

would see them plain as day. And the three nights I spent under those trees were no different than tonight. Same light, same moon, same shadows.

And I realized then that perhaps Hannah had seen me watching her. That perhaps she had wanted me to watch her.

I closed the window and turned back to the room. I climbed into the bed and slid my body as close to her as I dared. My knees behind her knees. She stirred slightly when I slung my arm around her. But soon her breathing became easy and regular. In this way sleep came for both of us.

We used to play this game. Where we'd press our faces together, as close as we could, my nose on her nose, my lips on her lips, my eyes in front of her eyes. We were so close we couldn't see anything. The winner was whoever could go the longest without pulling away. It was disorienting. Still, it drove Hannah crazy that I always won.

She'd say, "Next time I'll get you."

But she never did. I think maybe it's because she kept her eyes closed. It can be weird and blurry seeing someone else from that distance. But if you keep your eyes open, you get used to it after a while, and your breath slows, and then you begin to breathe like the one across from you. You forget that you're a separate person somehow. And when you forget this, there is no need to pull away. You're right where you belong.

She grew like a tree. As a little girl her hair was more blond than red. It was curly, too, and she was the cutest thing. She looked like Shirley Temple, not that you know who that is. She could have done commercials, she was that pretty. Those big green eyes. On the island she liked to make sand castles. There is a great picture of her standing at the edge of the water, a toy shovel in one hand, a toy bucket in the other. The surf is around her ankles. She has on this little bathing suit, the kind that has a skirt attached. Her legs are baby pudgy. And she's looking over her shoulder back at the camera. A streak of wet sand is on one cheek. She's smiling. The biggest smile you've ever seen. Even then she lit up everything around her.

Jacob taught her to ride a bike. I was so afraid of her falling. She seemed so small and fragile to me. Jacob said, she's a little girl, Irene, little girls are tough. I watched from the window as he supported her up and down the driveway. She was fearless and wanted to go on her own. I could barely watch. The look on her face was so serious, so determined. Jacob supported her and they picked up speed and then he let go. I could have killed him. But then she was moving fast, her little legs pedaling furiously. She went a good thirty yards before she fell. The bike tumbled and fell onto her. I raced out of the house and even beat Jacob to her. She was crying like mad and her leg was all scraped up. It's okay, baby, I told her. And Jacob said, Irene, she's fine. And she was. She was fine. Little girls get hurt but they don't break.

Hannah and I quickly fell into a routine. She worked during the days and I kicked around the beach. We met back at the house for dinner and wine. The weather seemed to mirror my mood, and we were blessed with a run of bright sun and warm nights. After we ate we sat outside and later we lay together in her large bed. We would kiss and then we'd hold each other and we never did more than that. We'd stay up talking until she fell asleep. And then I'd watch her until I grew tired.

One morning as she dressed for work, I lay in the bed and looked around the remarkable room. It was square where the door from the hallway led into it and then it curved outward until it reached the turret. The high ceiling had an ornate border. At its center a pattern of pale blue and gold swirled around the large light fixture. Walls painted an eggshell blue. A few minutes later, Hannah came to me and told me I had to get up.

"How 'bout I just wait for you to return?"

"Not today. The cleaning service comes."

"Come back to bed," I said.

"I have to go. I'm going to be late already."

I reached for her and she feigned like she didn't want me to but I pulled her down on top of me. "Stay," I said.

"I can't, Anthony. I have to go."

I kissed her forehead. "Come on."

She shook her head and broke free and stood up. "Don't stay in bed too long. They'll be here soon."

After Hannah left I closed my eyes, only for a moment, I told myself. But I fell asleep and when I woke I heard voices in the hallway. And they were not just any voices, but the voices of my home. Women with Portuguese accents.

I dove out of bed in only my shorts and I ran to the closet and slipped inside it, closing the door behind me. They were in the room now. The closet door was partly ajar but I didn't dare close it all the way. I had left my clothes on the bed, and my boots were on the floor.

There were two of them. Through the slightly open door I saw hands on the bed. I moved deeper into the closet, trying not to make any noise. Her clothes were all around me now, and I could smell her soap on them. It was a smell particular to Hannah, and I had already learned to love it. A figure passed by the door and then came back and I got a good look at her. It was Maria, a girl I had grown up with in Galilee. We had gone to school together from kindergarten until I dropped out after tenth grade. The other woman sounded older. I heard her say something and then Maria was out of sight. I pictured Maria. She had sweet brown eyes. Stocky-legged but pretty. The kind of girl Berta always wanted me to marry. I had not seen her in a while, though I knew her father. He was a fisherman on a small boat that caught pollock and other bottom-feeders for the big companies.

The older woman came into view and I did not know her.

She was short and heavy, curly dark hair in a hairnet. She held my shirt and my pants in her hand, lifting them up like they were garbage. She said, *"Algum tem estado se divertindomuito."* Someone's been having fun. I heard Maria laugh and then the sound of a vacuum. I exhaled.

I didn't move until I was certain they were gone. I never told Hannah about the close call, probably because I didn't want to remind her how different we were. That I grew up with her maids.

Later that same afternoon, I grew antsy with the same routine. I grew tired of the beach. I didn't want to fish anymore. I paced around at my camp smoking for a while and a darkness came over me. Maybe it was seeing Maria in that house. Wondering what Maria would have thought had she opened the door before I had a chance to wake and found me in the bed. Something about this idea soured the happiness I had been feeling. I paced around and I thought that it might be a good idea to go see Hannah. I didn't want to wait until the evening when she got home. I wanted to see her now, just to be pulled back to where I was before the maids shattered my sleep.

I had not been back to the village since I arrived on the island. I went to the general store near the lighthouse for food and cigarettes, but my only other interaction was with Hannah and the great house. The village was where Sheriff Riker was. And the roads were where Sheriff Riker patrolled in his car. But my need to see her that afternoon outweighed any concerns I had about running into him.

And so I walked that long island road again, as I had that first day. I wore my hat low over my eyes. I winced every time a car approached but the only cars I saw belonged to islanders and to tourists.

When I reached the edge of the village, I turned down one of the side streets. I had not bothered to ask her where the ice cream store was, but I knew there were only a few commercial blocks on the island. I didn't remember seeing it on the Main Street in front of the ferry but I thought this side street would lead me to the other set of stores that I did not pass that day. As it worked out, the store was on the side street itself, a small clapboard building next to other small clapboard buildings that housed clothing stores, delis, and little storefront restaurants. A small red sign had Benny's written across it in script.

When I opened the screen door, I did not see Hannah. There were two plain-faced girls that looked like sisters behind a wooden counter. The only customers were a family, a tall, athletic-looking man and his equally tall wife. Two blond boys. I went to the counter.

"Can I help you?" one of the plain-faced girls asked.

"I'm here to see Hannah."

The girl looked puzzled. I knew it was the way I appeared. Shorts with work boots on. Dark skin. She turned toward a room in the back I couldn't see and she called her name. In a moment Hannah came from the right, wiping her hands on a dishcloth. She could not disguise her feelings. I already knew her well enough to read her face. She did not light up with the sight of me. She did not want me here and when she smiled, it was weak and forced. To my right one of the plain-faced girls handed ice cream cones across the counter to the tall man. She whispered hello.

"Hey," I said.

"What are you doing here?"

"I came to visit."

She looked around. "I'm working."

"I needed to see you," I said.

Having gotten their change and their cones, the family made for the exit. The two plain-faced girls folded their arms over their chests and I knew they were studying me but I was ignoring them. I looked at Hannah, who seemed tight to me. One of the girls said, "Hannah, you going to introduce us to your friend?"

I gazed at the one who spoke. She smiled at me and pulled on one of her bangs over and over. "I have to go," Hannah said.

"You don't look busy."

She lowered her voice. "I have to go. I'll see you later, okay?"

I nodded. "You're embarrassed of me," I said.

"No," she whispered, shaking her head. "I just have to work."

"You are," I said. "Don't worry, I won't let them hear. But you're embarrassed of me."

She reached for my hand then, but I wasn't having it. "No, Anthony," she said.

Behind me the screen door opened and I turned to see several boys, twelve or thirteen years old, muscling their way into the store. The small space filled with their energy.

"Maybe I'll see you later," I said. "Maybe not."

I spun and walked out the door. I didn't pause to see if Hannah had followed me.

I did not go to the house that night. On the beach I leaned against the rock promontory and I watched the day turn into night. My anger left with the sun. Now I was just sad. I had shown her too much and too soon. I wondered if she would find me and I hoped that she would. I couldn't stand it if she didn't. I had revealed myself to her, and she needed to come to me.

Above me the last light bled from the sky. The tide rolled in. I smoked and I listened to it. And then Hannah came out of the shadows and stood over me where I sat and I didn't look at her. My heart lifted but I didn't want her to see this so I watched the tide.

"I'm sorry," Hannah said.

"Sit down."

She sat next to me and crossed her legs Indian-style. "I'm not embarrassed of you," she said.

"No?"

"No. I'm not."

"Could of fooled me," I said.

"Those girls aren't my friends."

"I don't care."

"It's a small town. I don't like people knowing what I'm doing."

"I shouldn't have just shown up," I said.

"I'm sorry," she said again.

"It's okay," I said, and it was. I was just happy Hannah had come to find me. For the first time, I wasn't chasing her anymore.

"Come here," I said, and she inched closer to me on the sand. I put my arm around her and she moved into me and we kissed. We kissed for a while and then we stopped. The dark came completely and we sat next to each other and when we started kissing again, we didn't stop. She rolled on top of me and on the bedroll her long hair swung in front of my face.

"We can if you want," she said.

"Okay."

"Do you have anything?"

"No."

"Don't come inside me."

I had no idea what I was doing and when she first moved on top of me I mistook the expression on her face for pain. But then she smiled at me and I knew it was going to be fine.

"Wait for me," Hannah said, and I didn't know what this meant. I held her shoulders in my hands and she slid on top of me and when I pushed her away, she rolled back like a wave.

"Like that," she said.

The night was black but I could see well enough to know when she closed her eyes. I thought that I should too but the truth was that I wanted to watch her face. It seemed as if every line on her skin, every tiny perfect freckle was there for me, because of me. I was suddenly aware of everything: the steady ebbing of the tide as it moved closer. The beach. The two of us, where we were joined. I tightened my hands on her shoulders, pressing down. She murmured yes and I gave in and shut my eyes and there was only Hannah, the softness of her skin underneath my palms.

After, when she had fallen into me and then rolled away, I wrapped my arms around her bare belly and I said, "I'm sorry."

"For what?"

"I can do better."

"It was perfect."

She spun into me then and rested her head on my chest. We looked up at the new stars. I ran my hands through her hair. I felt like talking. I said, "I always want it to be like this."

"Like what?"

"You in my arms."

"You're sweet."

"I'm in love."

She laughed at me. "Silly. It takes a long time to be in love."

"No, it doesn't."

"How do you know?"

"I do."

"Love at first sight?"

"Yeah," I said, and I didn't care if she knew it.

"Only in the movies," she said.

"No," I said. "Here. Now."

"When you first saw me you had just woken up. Maybe you were confused."

"I didn't know a girl could be so beautiful."

"Is that really what you thought?"

"I didn't know a girl could get more beautiful every day. That every time you see her you notice something different."

"Like what?"

"Like this," I said, and I moved her hair where it rested off to the side. I ran one finger along the nape of her neck. "How soft your skin is here."

"You're going to make me cry."

"I don't want you to cry."

"Then stop saying such nice things."

"Okay," I said. "No more nice things." I played with her hair. I slid my fingers through it and I massaged her scalp.

"That feels good."

And we lay in silence then. Somewhere in the distance a car made its way around one of the island roads, changing gears on the switchbacks. A reminder that there were other people in the world. Above I noticed now the first quarter moon, stuck in the branches of the overhanging trees. I pulled her tighter and soon she was snoring lightly and sometime after that I fell asleep too.

When I woke, the sky was subdued with the gray of dawn. A light fog had blown in off the water. It had cooled off and when I reached for Hannah I realized that she was already awake and had been crying. When she turned toward me, her eyes were rimmed with red.

"What is it?" I asked.

She shook her head. "It's nothing."

"Tell me."

She laid her head on my chest, away from me so that I could not see her face. "It's nothing," Hannah said again.

"*Garota bonita*," I said.

"What's that?"

"It's Portuguese."

"What's it mean?"

"Pretty girl."

"That's nice," she said. "Tell me something else."

I thought for a moment. I said, *"Eu morreria por voce."*

"What's that?"

"I would die for you."

She lifted her head and looked at me. Then she punched me in the chest with her small fist, not hard enough to really hurt but it stung anyway. She said, "Don't say that. Don't ever say that."

"Okay," I said.

"I mean it. Promise me."

"I won't say it."

She laid her head back down and her face was warm against my bare chest. The air was wet with the morning fog. I wondered what the day would bring. I wondered if it would rain. I ran my fingers through her hair and for some reason I suddenly imagined the beach in the winter, as I had seen it from sea. Snow-covered and windblown, the rocky cliffs slick with ice. In time Hannah fell asleep again but I did not. I watched the whitecaps rippling from east to west and I held her against the cold.

Berta visits me about once a month. She still lives in our small house and she still cooks at the college. At first she visited me more often but I know it's hard for her to come here and I understand that. She takes the bus from Galilee and has to switch buses three times before she gets here. In good weather we walk around the grounds and I hold her hand and we talk about nice things, simple things, like the weather, how the old town has changed since I was last there, the condos that have been going up near the harbor. Rich people moving into our working town. There's talk about large-scale development and someone has even made noise about buying every house in our neighborhood. Berta doesn't want that to happen, even though they would probably overpay for those small houses and she could live somewhere better. But I know she sees my father in that house, and me before all this happened, and she remembers happier times. Maybe she thinks those memories would go away if she left. I think we all reach a point in our lives where the memories are all we have to hang on to. We stop living, in a sense, except in our minds. I know what Dr. Mitchell would say about that, but I don't care. I like to picture Berta in front of the television in our house, sitting in the overstuffed chair, her eyes closed. But instead of sleeping, she reaches back across time and she remembers. She remembers my father and she traces their life together. All those moments when he made her laugh, how she felt when he opened the door after returning from sea and took her in his arms. And then she remembers bringing me into the world and even the little sister that I did not know. Maybe she pictures my father and me kicking the soccer ball back and forth in the sandy street. Father and son and the lives we had not yet led, the possibilities of everything unfolding in front of us like a map. Maybe she sees this and it warms her. Maybe it makes her happy and gives her solace. And maybe that is enough.

It's hard to believe that I was on the island for less than three weeks. I think we both realized—once we were into it—that it was not going to last forever. The funny thing was that we never talked about this. We never spoke of time, of when I would have to leave, of when she would have to leave. I had told her I had missed my boat and she never asked me another thing about it. I know now that Hannah didn't bring it up for the same reasons I didn't. To do so would have been to give it words, and giving it words would have made it real. Something we couldn't turn back from. I know you can't control time like that, but both of us thought we could. Or at least the days and the nights seemed longer when we ignored the obvious.

The sex was the newest part for me. I had been a virgin before I met Hannah, which I think she knew but I don't mind saying anyway. The passion of it surprised me. I was unprepared for how quickly it stripped away whatever remaining walls may have stood between us. I confess that a few times I found the whole thing stressful, since Hannah seemed to want more than I could give her. There was a line, I think, between what was loving and what was not. I was so new at all of it, so that when she would want me to pull on her hair until it hurt, I couldn't understand why she wanted me to hurt her.

"Just do it, Anthony," she demanded.

And so I did, though I did it reluctantly, and afterward, when we lay together in the quiet with our skin warm against each other, I sometimes felt bad about it all, like I had let her down, even though I was doing exactly what she had asked me to do.

The morning Hannah told me her mother was coming, a fog rolled in from the east and it brought the first rain we had seen since we had been together. At first it wasn't much more than drizzle but by midday it was pouring. It was a day Hannah didn't have to work and we spent the whole morning, as had become our habit, in bed. It seemed like we could have divided our life together into two parts: when we were having sex and when we had just finished. I remember that we were lying there watching the rain fall in a gray sky out the windows. I went to say something about it when she interrupted me.

She said, "My mother's coming."

"When?"

"Today."

She rolled away from me so I could not see her face and I looked again to the window and the rain that fell now like bars of silver. "Okay," I said.

"I should've told you sooner."

"Don't sweat it," I said.

"It'd be better if . . ."

"What?"

"I don't know how to say this," Hannah said.

"Tell me."

"If she didn't know about us."

"How long is she here?"

She turned back toward me. I brushed the hair away from her forehead. "The weekend," she said. "She hates it here, but she feels like she has to check on me."

"I'll be okay," I said.

"It's not what you think," Hannah said. "It's just that if she thought I was involved with a boy, any boy, she wouldn't leave. Then we couldn't be together."

"I get it," I said.

"Do you?"

"Yeah."

I watched the rain fall and wondered what I would do with myself if I had to stay away from the house. It was a soaking rain but maybe it would let up. She leaned in and kissed me then and we kissed for a while. Then she said, "It's only two nights."

I nodded. "Two nights will feel like a long time."

Her green eyes narrowed and then she smiled. "I'll miss you," she said.

"You sure?"

She nodded and her hair fell in front of her eyes and now she swept it away. But I was greedy for her, drunk for her, and every moment away from her felt empty. The truth was that sometimes it took another person to teach you how to be alive.

Later that afternoon the rain picked up and fell in sheets on the beach. It was so heavy that I could not see the water. I sat wedged under the rock face and I was miserable. My luck had run out. The promontory provided some shelter but it was not enough. When the wind blew the rain came right in and soaked my clothes. Hannah was with her mother by now. What were the two of them doing? They would have the great house to themselves. I would be stuck on the beach, the rain-soaked beach.

At least I was smart enough to snag two bottles of wine from the cellar before I left. I might be wet but I had the wine and that was a comfort.

I wished there was someplace I could go. I had money. I thought about getting a hotel room. Lying on a warm bed and watching television. But I didn't have a credit card and I knew you needed one for places like that. Besides, I didn't look like someone who belonged in a fancy inn. My presence might raise questions. A phone call to the sheriff.

So I sat and watched the rain. I was wet and cold. And I felt the sadness coming on. I felt it coming on like a cold.

When the wind shifted at dusk and the rain began to come sideways under the rock, I broke camp. I piled my things into the oilskin and made for the cove. Passing the overturned rowboats, for a moment I thought about using them somehow to build a shelter. But someone might notice them missing.

At the cove I started to walk up the trail that led to the house. I knew I could not go to the house. But halfway up the hill, where the trees started, it leveled off and the pitch pines grew closely together. I made my way into the grove, holding my right arm in front of me to keep stray branches from catching me in the face. In between two tall trees I stopped. The rain fell steadily here but it was not as bad as the exposed beach. I put my oilskin bag down. I removed my heavy raincoat. From my bag, I took out the good test fishing line. It took me a while in the new dark but I strung the coat between the trees. Tied it firm with the fishing line. I sat down under it. The rain pinged on top of the heavy rubber. But even though the pine needles below me were wet, the rain no longer fell on me. I stood and laid a towel on the pine needles. Then I took out my bedroll and laid it folded in half on top of the towel. I sat back down. This was much more like it. The rain couldn't reach me anymore.

I opened one of the bottles of wine. I drank straight from it. I lighted a cigarette. I was halfway up the cliff face. The path was to my left. To my right were more trees and the hilly land that led to the cliff walk. In front of me was the dark ocean obscured by the rain and the fog and the dark. Behind me was the house and inside it were Hannah and her mother.

I wondered what they had eaten for dinner. Surely more than the turkey sandwich from the general store that I had devoured as soon as I bought it. I wondered what Hannah talked about. If she was tempted to tell her mother about me, about how in two weeks we had grown closer than many people do in a lifetime. Mostly, I wondered if she looked to the window. If she looked to the window and the rain and worried about me. Worried about me sitting out here getting wet.

Maybe Hannah would come find me. When her mother fell asleep, I thought. Mothers went to sleep early. She probably couldn't wait. Of course, she'd look for me on the beach. But that'd be okay. I'd hear her on the path when she went by. No one else would be walking the path to the cove in a downpour. I'd surprise her. And then she'd join me under my tarp and we could share the wine and make love with the rain around us. She'd tell me how hard it was to be at the house knowing the whole time that I was down here.

The night moved on. The rain continued. The dark grew more dense. I had a lot of time to think. I couldn't see anything except for the flash of my lighter when I lit another cigarette. In the quick light I got a sense of rain and trees and water. Lots of water. Spilling off the raincoat above me to the ground. Then the dark shrunk around me. I thought of Victor and the story

I would have to tell him. I thought about his eyes, how big they would get when I told him all that happened. When I told him about having sex on the beach. What it was like to have such a beautiful girl move on top of you. No fucking way, Tony, he'd say. I'd tell him the whole thing. God's honest truth, Vic.

I'd have to get an apartment. One like Victor had. Then on weekends Hannah could come visit and we'd never leave bed. The only thing that would make us move would be hunger. We'd get up to eat and then return to bed. Or maybe we'd just eat in bed. Or not eat at all. For who needs food when you have a warm bed?

I missed Victor. Everything we did together. Our summer routine, those nights drinking beer on the jetty. Someone to talk to like a brother. Who understood me like a brother.

And I missed Berta. She'd be watching television by herself. And she'd fall asleep in front of it. Without me to wake her she'd come to in the middle of the night and groggily make her way upstairs.

I even missed the *Lorrie Anne*. It would be nasty out there tonight. Fishing in this kind of rain. The deck slick with it. But I also knew when you had the work you didn't notice the weather as much. You were too busy. Besides, they were good men. Big Al and Ronny. Carlos. Captain Alavares. Brothers of a different kind.

I stubbed out one cigarette and lighted another. I took a long pull off the bottle of wine. Come find me, Hannah. Come find me and take me away from this rain. Take me away from this silly homesickness. Take me somewhere warm where I can climb inside you.

I had no sense of time. I never wore a watch. It had been hours since the sun went down. Because of all the rain it seemed longer. There had not been much light in the day to begin with. It had to be around ten now. Ten or eleven. And no sign of Hannah. No footfalls on the path to the cove. She had not come to get me.

At one point my legs cramped and I stood out from under my jury-rigged tarp. The rain had slowed a little but still fell steadily. Mist rose up all around me in the dark grove of trees. The rain soaked my hair. Where was she? Hannah had not said anything about coming to me, but I didn't think she had to. It was implied. I knew her mother was there and could not know about me and I respected that. Well, I understood it anyway. But she couldn't be with her mother all the time. Don't mothers go to sleep?

I began to walk. I moved carefully through the pine trees, fending off low-hanging branches as I went. Some were heavy with rainwater and when I pushed on them it spilled off in a rush and fell on me like a shower. I didn't care anymore. I reached the trail and turned toward the house.

The path was muddy from all the rain. My boots sloshed through it as I climbed. Out from under the tree cover it was a heavy rain and I had to wipe it away where it ran into my eyes. To my right the ocean was hidden by the fog.

The ground leveled below me and I knew I was close. I came through the final stand of trees and in front of me now was the house. It was ablaze with light and through the mist and the fog it glowed orange. It was like I was seeing it through gauze and the effect was almost confusing. She only used the one light at night, the one in her room. I had never seen the house like this before. With the heavy fog and the falling rain and the fuzzy light, it was like walking through a dream.

I moved across the wet grass toward the house. The orange lights seemed to pulse with every step I took. Maybe it was the wine, but if I didn't know better I might have thought the house itself was alive. It looked like it was breathing in the fog.

When I got about sixty yards from the house, I stopped. Through the rain I could see into the floor-to-ceiling windows of the big ballroom on the first floor. The chandelier was on and the whole room was awash with light but I didn't see anyone. I moved forward and I was even with the house now, standing on the side of it, and the windows were right in front of me, close enough that I could see the whole room but far enough away that anyone looking out would not be able to see me. And as I watched, a tall, thin woman with long blond hair came into view. She wore a black T-shirt and white pants. This must be her mother, I thought. She was really beautiful. I thought maybe she was talking on the phone because she was pacing back and forth on the parquet floor and she seemed to be speaking, though I didn't see anyone else. Then I realized she wasn't on the phone because her arms dropped to her side. Then she raised one up high and brought it back down, as people do when they are making a point. I strained my eyes through the rain and the mist. And then behind her, half-in and half-out of the room, I saw Hannah.

She leaned against one of the large doors and was dressed as I had never seen her before. She had on a long dress, almost to her ankles, and her hair was up. She looked remarkable, to tell you the truth, but I didn't focus on that because I knew she was upset about something. I was too far away and Hannah was partially in the shadows so I could not tell if she was crying. But from her body language I saw that something was not right. Her arms were crossed over her chest and her head hung to one side and downcast toward the floor. Her mother moved back and forth in front of her. I wished I could hear what she was saying because it looked like she was really giving it to Hannah. I hated to see her upset. She seemed so sad. She wouldn't look up at her mother. At one point her mother just stopped and glared at her. And I saw Hannah shaking her head over and over and for the first time it occurred to me that somehow they might be talking about me. But how was that possible? She wouldn't have volunteered anything. She was clear about that. And as I was thinking about this, I looked to the other end of the ballroom and I realized that they were not alone.

He was against the far wall, the way he stood a mirror image of Hannah, though he looked more bored than distressed. His arms were crossed in front of his chest. He had on a white long-sleeve shirt and beige khakis and maybe this was why I had not seen him before. He blended in with the colors of the room.

But there was no mistaking that slicked-back hair and the leathery sun-beaten skin. Sheriff Riker.

You might have thought that my concerns right then were

about getting caught. That I would have immediately broke into a sprint back to the hillside in the rain to get my things and figure out where to hide. But seeing the sheriff made me realize that the only reason he was there, the only reason for the sadness Hannah wore in the very way she stood, was because of me. And if this were true, it meant that the sheriff knew I was the one on the stairs that night. He had told Hannah that I had killed her father.

I was not worried that this meant I could go to prison. Instead I was worried that all we had built in the time we had been together might fall apart. That Hannah might not want to see me anymore. That she might even hate me. And I could not live with that. I needed to reach her somehow, reach her without getting caught, and explain everything. How it was all a mistake, how important she was to me. I needed to lay it out for Hannah and pray that she understood.

I stood in the soaking rain and stared through the fog and into the tall windows. My eyes moved back and forth from Hannah to her mother to Sheriff Riker. At one point Hannah stepped out of the shadows and I saw how hard she was crying and her mother went to her and tried to hold her but she shrugged her off. Then Hannah extended one arm out and pointed toward the back of the house, toward the cove and the beach. When she did, Sheriff Riker brought his hand to his mouth and in the dark to my right, toward the front of the house, I suddenly heard the crackle of his voice, and, more alarming, a human voice in response, some twenty yards away from where I stood.

I took one step back, my boots sinking into the wet earth. I strained my eyes through the blackness and I heard the voice again and then another one. "This way," one of them said.

I couldn't see anything at all. The rain fell all around me. I was happy for the dense fog. I glanced back at the window and Hannah's mother held her now. The sheriff was gone. A beam of light swept across the trees behind me. I saw them. They were in the driveway. Two flashlights and then three. Voices. I turned toward the cove and in the fog I broke into a light jog. I looked over my shoulder at the lights. They were moving this way but not quickly. They did not know yet where I was. I started to run. I ran behind the house and across the wet lawn. I kept close to the tree line and it was so foggy it probably did not matter. I could have run right down the middle of the grass and there was no way they could have seen me. I reached the path and sprinted down it. The path was so muddy my boots made big sloshing prints in the dirt. The earth was so soft from the rain that they were deep impressions. This was a problem. If they shined their lights on the ground, they would know exactly where I went.

I did not have much time. I crashed through the grove of trees to my makeshift camp. I left the raincoat up between the trees but I grabbed the oilskin bag and returned to the path. I climbed back up toward the house, moving as fast as I dared, my eyes peeled ahead for any lights. When I reached the grassy lawn I looked ahead through the fog. The house was still lit like a Christmas tree but I did not see the flashlights or the sheriff's men. I got on my knees with the oilskin bag in front of me. I moved backward on the path, dragging the bag across my footprints as I went. It wasn't perfect but it seemed to be working. If they came while I was doing this, I would need to stand and sprint for the beach, hope for the best. But I made decent time. The path would have the wipe marks on it but no one would make those out until the morning, if then. My prints, on the other hand, would have been plain as day. I crawled backward and I slid the bag and I looked ahead and I listened. The bag made a scraping sound as I went. The rain continued to fall. I worked as fast as I could. Any moment I expected to see flashlights moving on the path above me. But I made it to where my makeshift camp was and I lifted the bag and went through the trees. I sat again under my raincoat and I listened.

I wanted a cigarette so badly. Now that I was no longer moving, my heart raged in my chest. There was the rain and the heavy fog and the sound of my breathing. I did not hear anything else. Maybe they weren't looking for me at all. Maybe they were after something else altogether. I mean, I didn't know for sure that the sheriff had discovered somehow that I was the one in the house that night. I'll give it ten more minutes, I thought, then I'll have a cigarette. That'll calm me down.

A moment later, I heard them. I sucked in my breath and held it. They were on the path. Two, maybe three, men. Loud voices. I looked to my right through the dark and the rain. I couldn't see anything. Then I saw the fuzzy yellow glow of a flashlight in the fog. It was gone and then there it was again. There would be no reason for them to come in here, unless they saw my footprints or the drag marks from the bag. I released my breath and held it again. I heard them clearly now. They were even with me on the path. I saw two beams of light. One of them said, "How much farther?"

"It's got to be right here," the other said.

Then they were gone. I exhaled. I sat still until my legs began to cramp. I shifted and stretched them out in front of me. I stared into the blackness. I didn't dare move. I had nowhere to go.

Sometime before dawn the rain stopped. I only noticed it when I realized it had grown quieter. At first I didn't attribute it to the rain. It had been over an hour since the men took what I think was their third pass on the trail that led to the cove. I had spent my time trying to stay awake. Now and again I caught myself drifting off where I sat under the raincoat. Once when I woke I noticed the silence. The only water falling was the drip from the branches above. I spent my time considering my options. My only goal was to reach Hannah. I knew I could not go to the house. I wished I could get to a phone. I would call Victor and find out what they knew. I thought about trying to steal a skiff from one of the two island harbors. Piloting it back to the mainland. But then it occurred to me that if they were looking for me like this, they already had Victor. And Berta knew they were looking for me. And Captain Alavares too. Returning to the mainland wouldn't do me a lick of good.

My time was running out here. Soon it would be light and when it was light I would not be able to hide anymore. They would bring more men and maybe even dogs. Regardless, they would find me and when they did the jig would be up.

All I wanted to do was to see Hannah. I thought if I could see Hannah then maybe everything would be okay. If they found me, there was no way they would let me see her. But maybe if I went to them, it would be different. Maybe I could make a deal. I will talk to you, tell you what you want to know. In return, I want to be alone with Hannah. Let me explain all that happened. Let me tell her how much I love her, and how love can trump anything, even this.

I allowed myself the cigarette I had denied myself for the last five or six hours. I took my time and savored it. Through the trees in front of me the night was starting to lift. The fog was still heavy but things were turning from black to gray. I smoked and I took solace in the fact that at least I was going to the one place where Hannah was. I didn't know what other choice I had.

discovered something new about fear that morning. As I have said before, I had been afraid many times. Both at sea and on land. But my fear in the past had always been somehow tied to choice. I could choose to jump off the bridge with Victor to the waiting water. I could choose to not show up for the boat and the trip to the Grand Banks. Though, of course, once at sea there was not a lot I could do. The ocean was going to dictate what happened to all of us. But that morning, walking up the trail from the cove to the great house for the last time, I was not afraid. That's the honest truth. A sense of calm and resignation came over me. And I think that's because all the choices I had made led to this one place, this one lonely walk across rain-soaked earth.

What transpired next was something straight out of a movie. I emerged out of the heavy fog from the side yard of the great house to find a driveway filled with police cars. Sheriff cars, state police cars, a large white van. Men stood in small groups talking. I saw Sheriff Riker leaning against one car sipping coffee out of a styrofoam cup talking to three state troopers. There were men in suits. No one saw me. I stopped at the edge of the grass. All of them were engrossed in conversation. I took a deep breath, and then I shouted, "I want to see Hannah."

Everyone stopped talking all at once. All heads turned toward me. Time seemed to grind to a halt for a moment. They all just looked at me. And I must have been a sight, sitting in the rain all night. I thought about shouting my request again, as if they did not hear me the first time. But then Sheriff Riker stepped forward from everyone else and he calmly said my name. "Anthony," he said. "Let us see your hands, okay, buddy?"

And just like in the movies, I slowly raised my hands over my head. I opened my palms for them all to see. "I want to see Hannah," I said again.

"One thing at a time," Sheriff Riker said. "I need you to do me a favor, Anthony, understand?"

I nodded.

"Get down on your knees now, Anthony. Keep your hands above your head, just like that. But get down on your knees."

I did as he said. I slumped to the ground onto my knees and my oilskin bag slid off my shoulder and I let it fall next to me.

"Okay," the Sheriff said. "Just stay there, Anthony. Two of the officers are going to come to you now. Nod if you understand."

It seemed pretty clear that I understood since I went to my knees but I nodded anyway. Two of the state troopers, huge men in gray uniforms with jackboots, came toward me from the driveway. When they reached me they did not say anything. One of them took my hands from above my head and he pulled them down behind my back and I felt the cuffs go on, heard them snap into place. The morning was coming on but not yet here, the fog still heavy and the air the color of pigeons. The ocean was right there but you couldn't have seen it if you wanted to. I was on my knees, two troopers looming above me. I looked over at the house. Men talked all around me but to me it was all empty chatter. My eyes flitted up the façade to the turret window. No light on inside. No sign of Hannah anywhere. The empty glass in the rising misty morning didn't reflect a damn thing.

She had such a good heart. In some ways she was an innocent about things. She didn't know how the world worked. When she was only twelve, she got off the school bus one afternoon. The bus stop was only a half mile from our house in Chestnut Hill. There were six children who all got off at that stop and from there it was only a short walk from the main road to our neighborhood. It was a different time and the parents did not meet the children at the bus stop. Today I suppose that would be unthinkable. But the children were always in a group and it was a wealthy neighborhood once they were off Route 9.

This afternoon, standing on the corner of Route 9 and Silbey Street, was an older man with long gray hair and a beard, an army jacket that had patches all over the sleeves. A homeless gentleman. He held a sign toward the passing traffic that said, will work for food.

She was so young, so naïve, that she marched right up to the man. She told him she didn't have any work but that there was plenty of food at her house. A refrigerator full of it. I cannot imagine what the other kids thought. But when I opened our door and saw this man standing there, I almost had a heart attack. When I recovered from my shock, I had him wait on the steps while I made him a sandwich. I put it in a brown bag and handed it to him. Hannah was quite pleased, of course. I explained to her when he had left why what she had done was dangerous. And how she was never to do it again. But I couldn't possibly punish her for it. For how can you punish a child for showing generosity of spirit?

They took me off the island on the ferry, though this time I rode in its belly, in the back of a state police car. Before I got in they removed the handcuffs, which I was grateful for. Other than that, they left me alone in the backseat. The two troopers carried on like I wasn't there, talking about the Red Sox, the weather, some new restaurant in Providence. I stared out the window and through the breaks in the iron walls of the boat to where I could see patches of gray ocean.

We drove off the boat and then through the village and past my house and to the barracks in Westerly. They brought me into a small room with a table and two chairs. They left me there for a while and then Sheriff Riker and a tall man in a suit who introduced himself as a state police captain came in. He said his name was Martini.

"Like the drink," I said.

He smiled. "Like the drink."

And that was pretty much the last thing I said that afternoon. Sheriff Riker did most of the talking and he had lots of questions but all I did was stare straight ahead. I heard what he said but I didn't really listen. I discovered that if I actually listened then I felt a greater pressure to respond. But if I tuned him out and thought of other things—of Hannah mostly, of how she looked after we made love, the open O of her mouth, the tiny freckles on her cheekbones, the smooth length of her neck—I could forget they were there. It was a neat trick, and one I didn't know I could pull off until I was in that small room. I shut down and they knew I was doing it and there was nothing they could do about it.

Not that they didn't try. What I did glean from what they had to say was that Victor had confirmed that I was in the house that night. They broke him somehow and when they called the *Lorrie Anne* they found out I had never gone out. But the sheriff kept saying that he thinks I didn't mean for anything to happen. That there was no intent on my part.

"I know you're a good kid, Anthony," he said. "Work with me a little, okay? I want to consider this an accident but we need your help. If you won't talk to us we're in a tough position. We might have to assume some things you won't want. There's still time to fix this."

And on and on.

I stared blankly and didn't say a thing. After a time they left me and I was alone in the room for what seemed like hours. It was hard to tell. There were no clocks and nothing to do and each minute just yielded to the next one. Eventually the door opened and Berta walked in. It felt like forever and I was awfully glad to see her. Though she looked so sad, so concerned, that I had to fight not to cry. I stood and stepped out from the table and I hugged her hard. Berta gripped my T-shirt in her hands.

"It's all right, Mama," I said.

"What did you do, Anthony? Is this true, what they say?"

I looked toward the mirror that covered one of the walls. I knew they were on the other side looking at us. Could probably hear every word we said too.

"I'm in love, Mama," I said.

Berta looked up at me and let go of my shirt. She stepped away. "You stupid boy," she said. "You don't know anything."

"I know this much," I said.

Berta started to cry. I hated to see her cry more than anything and I tried to hug her but she was really upset. I started to cry too when she flailed at me with her short arms. She punched me with her little fists. "I'm in love, Mama," I said again, and she only cried harder but she let me hold her now, which I did until the door opened and Sheriff Riker walked in.

"It's time, Mrs. Lopes," he said.

My mother put her hands on my shoulders and looked up at my face. I looked down at her sweet wet brown eyes. "It's okay," I said, but Berta stared back at me like she didn't believe me anymore.

They came in and out all afternoon and still I did not talk. I thought about telling them that I wanted to see Hannah, telling them that I'd say whatever they wanted if only they'd let me see her. But part of me knew that there was no way, regardless of what I said, that they were going to let this happen. Finally, after I had been there for what seemed like ten hours, the door opened and in walked a man in a dark suit. I recognized him right away as he was from Galilee. He was maybe twelve years older than Victor and I. He had been a basketball star at the high school, the son of a fisherman like us, and he went away to college unlike us. Everyone knew him when we were kids. Girls loved him. And he looked exactly the same. Other than the streaks of silver coming in on his black hair above the ears. Danny Pedroia.

"You Anthony?" he said.

"Yes," I said.

"I'm your lawyer."

"My lawyer?"

"Court-appointed."

"I remember you," I said.

He flashed a big smile. He was used to this. "We're from the same town," he said. He held out his hand. "Dan Pedroia."

I shook it. "Anthony Lopes."

"Mind if I sit down?"

I motioned to the seat like it was my own house. He sat down across from me. I pulled my chair out and he did the same. I saw him studying me. "So," I said.

"First thing we have to do is get you out of here," he said.

"That'd be good."

"They're going to arraign you on Monday. I can't do anything before then. I'm sorry about that. They're going to keep you in a holding cell until then."

"Then what?"

"Then we go before a judge. I'm going to ask that you be released on your own recognizance. It just means you get to go home while we wait for trial."

"I know what it means," I said.

"Good. Or a plea, depending on what we decide to do. We make the case that you have strong ties to the community and are not a risk to flee. I'm going to say you'll agree to wear a monitor on your ankle and stay home. They're worried you'll try to find Ms. Forbes. But if the judge agrees, you get to live at home pending the outcome of the trial. If he disagrees he can set bail for you to go, in which case we'd need money to get you out. Or he may just leave you here until the trial."

I nodded. "Let's hope he agrees."

Danny Pedroia smiled. He had the smile of a shark but I liked him. He said, "I'm going to do what I can. One other thing I'm going to ask for. I want to have you evaluated."

"Evaluated?"

"See an expert. Someone you can talk to. Talk about the

time you spent on Cross Island. What brought you there. That kind of thing."

"I've been trying not to talk about it," I said.

"I know. That's good. This is different. It's smart right now not to say anything to the police. I'm talking about a psychiatrist. It could help."

I smiled. "Okay, Danny," I said.

Danny smiled when I used his neighborhood name. "Let's see if we can get you out of here, Anthony," he said.

After that, they gave up on me. They put me into a small holding cell somewhere in the state police barracks. There were two cells and both were empty. They put me in the far one and in it was a cot with a blanket and hard pillow. The toilet also doubled as a sink, which was something I had never seen before. They fed me twice a day. Pizza at night and a fast-food breakfast sandwich in the morning. Other than that, they did not bother me and I slept like I only did when I had the flu. I drifted in and out of dreams. A few times I woke in a cold sweat. I knew I had been having nightmares but I did not remember them. I'd sit on the edge of the cot and wish they'd let me smoke. Then I'd start to think about Hannah and it made me sad. I'd lie back down and sleep again because it was only in the sleeping that the sadness went away.

Monday morning they handcuffed me again and led me out the back of the barracks and into another police car. They drove me to the courthouse and inside they took off my cuffs and escorted me into a courtroom. Danny Pedroia was here as was Berta. I sat between them and we waited for our docket to be called. Berta's eyes were rimmed with red and she looked tired and old. My heart went out to her and I held her hand. Danny Pedroia talked into my ear, explaining everything that was happening, and when our number was called, the two of us stood and made our way to the front tables. We stood in front of the judge, who was old and black and bald with a gray mustache, and the prosecutor explained the charges against me, how serious they were, and the judge looked impassively at him as he did. Danny Pedroia explained that I was a good kid who did a dumb thing but had never done anything before. That I was from Galilee and that it was all I had ever known. That I was a fisherman and that my father had been a fisherman. Danny Pedroia was a good talker and I liked listening to him. He said I should be released on my own recognizance and undergo a competency evaluation. That I was no threat to anyone or even to myself. And that I certainly would not flee, that all my roots were in Galilee and there was nowhere for me to go. That I would be willing to wear an ankle monitor as an act of good faith.

"What about Cross Island?" the judge wanted to know.

"The young woman is no longer there," Danny said, and I perked up at this. "She left the island," he said, and I wanted to ask where Hannah went but I knew enough to know I couldn't do that.

The judge took all this in. He looked wise when he nodded as he listened. I thought that he was what a judge should look like. The prosecutor made another argument for bail. No one mentioned the money. They knew nothing about that. The judge shook his head. "I'm going to grant the defense request," he said.

And so that afternoon, for the first time in weeks, I returned home to my small bungalow. It was just me and Berta in the house. I had this small bracelet around my ankle with a little black box on it. If I left my small yard, or took the bracelet off, an alarm would sound and the police would come to get me. I stayed in my room mostly and smoked. At night I took in the late-August breeze and smelled the ocean from my window. In a couple of days the psychologists were going to come to my house. They were going to want to know if I was crazy. Danny Pedroia made it sound like it would be a good thing if they thought I was.

Dr. Mitchell likes to say that therapy is not a fix in itself. He says it's about giving me the tools to know how to handle situations, and how to make good choices. I've been through so much of it, I can say that the only thing I've been able to absolutely determine about it is that if you tell them what they want to hear, they will leave you alone. It doesn't mean you're cured, or that there was anything wrong with you in the first place. It just means they got the answers they wanted all along and if you pay attention you can usually figure what those are. You don't have to believe in what you're saying. You just need to say it.

Though, in that first week I was under house arrest, I had not yet learned this. I told them the truth about me and Hannah. I did not hide anything and I did not hold anything back. I just let it fly and hoped for the best.

There were two psychologists, a man and a woman. They were both youngish and seemed to always dress in brown. His name was Mike and hers was Diane and this was what they wanted me to call them. They came every morning and stayed for three hours each time. I told them about Victor and me riding my skiff to the island that night. How we thought the house was empty. I told them about finding the money. Seeing Hannah on the stairs. The tussle with her father. I told them how I kept seeing her in my dreams and then sometimes when I was awake. I told them I saw her reflected in the eye of a fish. I told them all I wanted to know was the color of her eyes and when I told them this they both nodded like it was the most natural thing in the world. I said that when I saw her high above me on the ferry I knew that I had no choice but to go to the island and find her. I spoke of watching Hannah through the window. They wanted to know if she knew I had done this and I told them I couldn't be sure, which was the truth, but I also told them it didn't matter.

"Why's that, Anthony?" Diane asked, leaning forward as if this was important.

"It's just not the point," I told her. "What counts is not what led to us being together, but the fact that we were together. And how perfect it was."

Sometimes when I talked they took notes, but mostly they just listened. One morning they gave me a series of tests. They had me rearrange blocks and they had me look at blotches of ink and tell them what I saw. I had a hard time taking this seriously, like this had anything at all to do with me and Hannah, so I thought of the craziest things I could and said them. "It looks like two bears fucking," I said when I looked at one that really looked like nothing at all.

In the afternoons I watched television until Berta came home. Then we had dinner. Other than that, we moved around each other like ghosts, both of us pretending that nothing had changed, and both of us knowing better. My mother didn't understand me and I knew enough to know that I could not expect her to. In the evenings I sat on the windowsill in my room and looked at the small neighborhood and smoked. This was the hardest time for me. In the air I could feel summer disappearing. Below a few leaves were already on the ground. I felt completely alone.

At night the neighborhood was dead still. Small houses full of hardworking people who slept when it grew dark. You could hear the occasional car out on the main road and sometimes the foghorn from the lighthouse but otherwise it was quiet.

The fourth night I was back I heard something that sounded like the scuff of a shoe on the pavement and when I looked toward the road, I saw a figure in the pooling lamplight. It didn't matter that I couldn't make out anything but the shape. I knew who it was. He moved toward the yard and from below me he whispered my name.

"Tony," he said.

I know I was supposed to be angry with him. He had told the sheriff everything. But it was Victor and he was a brother and regardless of how mad I should be, I was really happy to see him.

"Can you come down?" he asked.

"Hang on," I said.

Victor had a brown bag and inside it were two forty-ounce bottles of beer and we sat down against the outside wall of my house and drank the beer and talked. Victor told me how they trapped him. Apparently, when going through the lists of all the people who had visited the house on the island, from gardeners to electricians, they saw his name on the list from the funeral home. From there it was simply a matter of telling Victor that I had already confessed. He told them the whole thing.

"I'm really sorry, man," he said.

"It's all right," I said.

"They never arrested me," he said. "They said they only would if I didn't testify against you. They were much more interested in you. They wanted to know where you had gone. I had no idea and that's what I told them. I can't believe you were crazy enough to go out there. When I heard that was where they found you, I almost shit my pants. I thought, fucking, Tony. He's lost it."

I told Victor all about Hannah then, every part of it, well, almost every part. A few things I kept to myself, which was how it should be. I told him all that I could about Hannah, and when I was done, Victor said, "Shit, man, you got it bad."

I said, "I need your car."

"What? What for?"

"I need to find her."

Victor shook his head in the dark next to me. "You really are loco, man. No way. I can't do that."

"Come on, Vic," I said. "I'm not going to take Berta's."

Victor tipped his head back as he drank from his beer. He lighted a cigarette and I lighted one off of his. "Tony, I can't. They'll get me for that. You got to forget about this crazy talk. Danny Pedroia told my mother that this can be settled. You're going to screw that all up."

I looked over at him. "You going to help me or not?"

"Aren't they keeping track of you or something? They'll find you in two minutes."

I showed Victor my ankle then. "I'll just cut it off. By the time they get here, I'll be gone."

"You've lost it."

"I have to do this."

"What am I supposed to tell them? That I give you my car?"

"Nah," I said. "When they find out, tell them I just took it. That I knew where you kept your keys. You had no idea."

Victor didn't respond to this right away. We both drank again from our beer and we looked to the street and where the streetlights cast their yellow light. The air already smelled a little of fall. I finished my cigarette and I knew I didn't have to say anything else, that Victor was going to give me the car, because he was my brother and I had told him what I needed to do. I was going to find her and he was not going to get in the way.

Victor did two things for me the following night. First, he left his old Chevy sedan in front of my house. And second, on the front bench seat, was a map of New England and on it he had drawn in red a line from Galilee, Rhode Island to Lincoln, Connecticut. He had done exactly what I asked him to do. Gone to the library and found out where her school, Miss Watson's, was. And brought me the directions to find it.

I waited until midnight, smoking in my bedroom window. My oilskin bag was already packed, as it had been when I left for the island. I had no idea how long it would take the police to respond when I cut the bracelet. There would not be many cars on the road this time of night and that was a risk. Though I thought it would be easier to go in the dark. I thought they would take longer to get here. Besides, they didn't have any reason to think I'd be in a car. They'd probably check my skiff first, and by that time, I might have already crossed state lines.

Before I left, I stopped for a moment in front of Berta's room. The door was slightly ajar and I could see her on the bed. She often slept like she was in a coffin, on her back, her short arms crossed on her chest. She was like this tonight and I stood in silence and watched the slow rise and fall of her breath. This was going to hurt her, my doing this, and I knew that in no time at all a pounding on the door would awaken her. Then the house would be full of state police. It broke my heart to do this to her, but I no longer felt like I had a choice.

I made my way down the stairs and then to the front door. I walked out and into the night. In the front yard, I stopped and looked up through the trees to the sky. It was overcast and there was no starlight or moonlight, just a low black ceiling. I put my bag on the ground and unzipped it and took out my fishing knife. I got down on one knee and I put the blade under the bracelet. The knife was sharp and it took one quick tug and it was off. I stood and tossed it over my shoulder and ran for the car.

I put my bag on the seat and turned the ignition and it started right up and I drove off through the still neighborhood. There was a shortcut that would take me on back roads out toward Route 1 and I took this, wanting to stay away from the harbor and the obvious routes.

I drove past the small darkened houses, many of them with skiffs in the driveways, fishing equipment on the lawns. I drove quickly but not too quickly and soon I reached the state highway and I turned onto it and I was the only car. I drove north, away from the coast. I kept looking in my rearview mirror but there was nothing. Then, from in front of me, I saw them coming at me, two state troopers, lights flashing. They passed by me, heading toward Galilee, and I breathed in deep when we passed, looking back to see if they were turning around, but they did not.

Soon I reached Route 1 and there were other cars out here and I relaxed a little bit. I stayed around the speed limit. Victor's car was a hunk of junk, but it had a valid inspection sticker and everything essential worked. There was a good deal of rust around the wheels and the upholstery on the backseat was all torn up. But it drove okay as long as you didn't try to go too fast. Then the wheel shook underneath your fingers and it felt like it was tough to control.

My goal that night was to get out of Rhode Island. It sounds funny to say it now, but I had never been out of Rhode Island before. Unless you count on a boat, in which case I had almost been to Greenland.

I reached Providence an hour later and cars were whizzing by me on either side now. Victor's radio didn't work so the only sound was the highway, the engine, the other cars. I felt my mood brightening in a way it had not since I had last seen Hannah. I was moving again and there was something freeing about taking action, being in control of things. I had the car and the road and I could make my own decisions. And I was coming to find Hannah. This was the most important thing of all.

trouble sleeping and

At two in the morning, I crossed into Connecticut on Route 6. First there was a sign that said leaving Rhode Island and then another welcoming me to Connecticut. I went through the center of a few small towns, deserted at this time of night, and then into a pine forest. I had the window down as I smoked and the air was silent and still and cool. The sky had cleared as I moved inland and a half-moon showed between drifting clouds above. I was the only car on the road and for a moment I thought about killing my headlights, rolling down the other windows, and becoming as much a part of the night as I could.

I slept in a small state park, driving the car down a narrow tree-lined road to a parking area that looked abandoned. I put the car in the far corner under the cover of large pines. With the dark car and the shadows it would have been hard to see unless you shined a headlight right on it. Now that I was no longer driving, I was bone-tired. I laid my bedroll out on the backseat of the car and used the rest of my bag as a pillow. I kicked off my boots and tried to get comfortable. The space was too small for my limbs but for the first time in a while, I had no trouble sleeping. I don't even remember slipping under. One

moment I was looking through the back window at the trees and
the sky and the next thing I knew bright sunlight rained down
on me. It was a dreamless night and that was how tired I was.
The day came before I knew it.

In a small town I found a McDonald's and pulled through
the drive-through and got coffee and a sandwich. I ate on the
road, which led me up and over soft rolling wooded hills. It was
a nice day, sunny and mild. Now and again I looked at the map,
but mostly I just drove. I liked driving, I decided, especially on
a nice day. The truth was I didn't really know where I was going.
I knew where her school was but I had no idea if she would be
there. I had no idea when school started and my worst fear was
that because of all that had happened, that Hannah might have
changed plans somehow. But Miss Watson's was all I had to hang
my hat on, and from the map it looked like I would be crossing
practically the whole state of Connecticut to get there.

I drove through small farm towns that looked like they
could have been anywhere. And then through towns with greens
where all the old houses seemed to be white and the churches
were too. Then into the glass towers of Hartford and back out
again. Crossing the Connecticut River and back to small towns,
more woods and hilly land. And finally, in the late afternoon, I
drove down the country highway and into the town of Lincoln,
home of Miss Watson's.

I don't know what I expected but there wasn't much to the
place. The land was pretty, I'll say that. Mountainous com-
pared to what I was used to. Narrow roads and steep hills. Tons
of woods. But beyond that the town seemed to consist of this
one road, a few stores, nice older homes right on the road, and
then the school itself, a mass of brick buildings on both sides
of it, surrounded by open fields and forest. I decided I would

just drive by the school the first time. I slowed down passing it and the place seemed empty. In front of one of the buildings I did see a police car and this got me worried that maybe they figured out this was where I was heading. The car looked empty, though. But I didn't see any students, or any people at all, other than one fat guy cutting grass on a riding mower and an older couple walking a dog.

It was still August. I figured school had not started yet, but I knew it wouldn't be long. I needed a place to hunker down and wait. I needed to be patient.

I drove past the school and several towns away, on the same rural highway, I came upon a campground. It cost five bucks a night and had showers and bathrooms and the guy running the office showed zero interest in me. He barely looked up when I paid in advance for a week. There were a few other people camping there, but mostly it was empty. I picked a spot deep in the back and against the woods and next to a small brook. It could not be seen from any of the campsites in use. I didn't have a tent and the last thing I needed was someone raising questions about me. I was too close for that to happen.

some firewood from the ear...

In the mornings I drove those winding roads to the nearest good-sized town, Litchfield, and I ate either McDonald's or Burger King and then I drove by the school to see if anything was happening. The place was deserted. Occasionally someone who looked like a janitor or a maintenance person was walking around but that was it. No students that I could see. There was also no sign of the police car I had seen the first time I drove by and this made me feel better. No doubt half of Rhode Island was looking for me, but they hadn't figured to look here yet. Though perhaps that was only because Hannah had not arrived.

With my one piece of work taken care of, I had nothing to do but kill time. Once I went to a matinee movie at the theater in Litchfield, which took up most of the afternoon, but I knew I couldn't do that every day. There weren't a lot of Portuguese boys my age in that town and like on Cross Island, I stood out. The rest of the days were interminable, to tell you the truth. I sat around my campsite and thought about home, and about Hannah, and about everything that had happened. I bought some firewood from the camp office and at night I built a fire

and at least this was something to look at. I'd watch the burning logs for hours, stirring the coals with a long stick. I wished
I had some beer or wine but I didn't. I smoked cigarettes until
I got so tired there was nothing left to do but curl up on my
bedroll and go to sleep.

My third day there, I returned back to the campground
to discover that the campsite closest to me was now occupied.
It was through some thin poplars and also next to the brook.
Parked there was a rusty pickup truck and one of those small
popup campers in front of which, on a lawn chair, sat an old
man with gray hair as long as a woman's. It came down either
side of his face and partway down his chest. He had an ample
belly. It wasn't even noon yet, but he had an open can of beer
and a cigarette. He waved to me when I pulled up and I waved
back. I got out of the car and stood at my meager site trying to
figure out what to do about this guy who would soon know that
I didn't have a tent. That I was sleeping on the ground or in
my car. I didn't know much about camping, but the one thing I
knew is that no one slept on the ground intentionally. You were
on the run from something, most likely, and were probably
someone to be avoided.

And as I stood next to the brook thinking this, the old man
called to me. I didn't hear what he said but I knew he was addressing me. I turned and looked at him through the small
trees and he was raising his can of beer at me. I heard him
clearly now. He said, "Have a beer."

I wasn't one to drink in the morning but I also didn't know
how to say no to that. I walked through the trees to his campsite and when he saw me coming he stood and climbed into
his small camper. I didn't know what to do so I stopped but a
moment later he emerged and he had another lawn chair.

"Come on, sit down," he said. He had a deep voice, gruff-sounding but friendly enough. I went over to him and was going to shake his hand but he just motioned at the chair. It was only about a foot away from him and facing the same way, toward my campsite, so that to look at him, I had to turn sideways. He handed me a beer and said, "I'm Terrence."

"Anthony. Thanks."

When I took the beer, I got a better look at him. He wore a white T-shirt and jean shorts, wool socks and sandals. His wrist had a tattoo of an anchor and on his calves, veins as thick as noodles stuck out of his skin.

"Some day, Anthony," he said.

I looked up at the blue sky over the woods. "Yeah," I said.

"You just passing through?" he asked.

For some reason I told him the truth. "I'm waiting for a girl."

Terrence laughed at this. "Waiting for a girl? Doesn't seem a great place for that."

"She goes to the school the next town over."

"The one on 75?"

"That's it," I said.

Terrence took a cigarette out and lighted it and I got one of my own and did the same. "I should be working," he said. "But I just got here. Take a day off and start tomorrow."

"What kind of work?"

"Mushrooms," he said. "Yup. I harvest mushrooms."

"For real?"

"Oh, yeah. These hills are full of 'em. And if you get the right ones, they're worth a pretty penny."

"So you just go into the woods and look for them?"

"No, no, there's much more to it than that." He pointed

to his head. "You got to use this. Know where they're hiding. What kind. Chanterelles and oysters, lobster mushrooms, hen-of-the-woods, you name it."

"Hen-of-the-woods?" I said.

"Yup. Those are huge. Found one at the base of an old tree a few miles from here last year. Thing barely fit in the bed of my truck. Got three hundred dollars for it from a restaurant owner in New York. That was a good day. Bought a lot of beer that did."

"I bet," I said.

"Anyway," Terrence said, and for a moment we sat in silence. I had not really talked to anyone since Victor came into my small yard in Galilee and I realized how much I missed other people. Then Terrence said, "What do you do when you're not waiting for a girl, Anthony?"

"I'm a fisherman," I said.

"Yeah? Where's that?"

"Galilee, Rhode Island."

"Ah," he said. "Know it well."

"You do?"

Terrence pointed to his wrist, and the tattoo of the anchor. "Merchant Marines. Twenty-five years. I been in and out of that old harbor more than a few times."

"I work on a swordboat," I said.

"That's some work," he said.

"Yeah," I said, "I miss it."

"That's what girls will do to you," he said. "Mess up what you like. I travel light myself. Of course I'm not your age anymore. I used to wait for girls, myself."

"This girl is worth it," I said.

Terrence reached down to the cooler underneath his chair

and brought out two more beers. "Drink up," he said, and I drained the rest of that first beer and took the second one from him. "Drink up and tell me about her."

I looked over at him. I saw his eyes for the first time clearly and they were the strangest shade of gray. I looked at his tattoo and his long hair and then I looked beyond him to his rusty pickup truck. And I thought that there are whole bunches of people that nobody knows about who live outside of normal things. Men who live on their own terms and make a living how they can, even if it means picking mushrooms in the woods. Who go where they want and when they want. Who answer to only themselves. Terrence was one of these men and I realized sitting next to him drinking beer in the morning that I was too.

I said, "She's something."

"What do you like about her the most?"

"Her eyes," I said. "Maybe her freckles."

Terrence nodded. "The eyes. What color?"

"Green. But not just any green. Bright. Beautiful."

"What color is her hair?"

"Kind of red. More blond. It changes with the sun."

"I like that," said Terrence. "Especially redheads."

"Yeah, it's nice."

"How about her titties?"

I laughed. "Her titties?"

Terrence smiled. "She got titties, don't she?"

"Yeah," I said, though I didn't really like the question.

"How are they?"

"They're fine," I said, a little firmly.

"Is she skinny or fat?"

"She's skinny."

Terrence made a *hrmph* sound. "I like a little meat on mine," he said. "Some cushion, you know what I mean."

I drank from my beer. I had a sudden feeling of not wanting to be there anymore. I looked over at Terrence and I saw him differently now, less benign, and I knew it was because I didn't like him talking about Hannah like that. He didn't know her and it was none of his business what she looked like. But there was something Terrence could do for me that I couldn't for myself.

I said, "Terrence, what do you think about buying me some beer? My money. I buy, you fly. Some to buy some for yourself too."

His eyes narrowed. "How old are you?"

"Seventeen."

He pulled on one side of his long hair. "I took you for older. All right," he said. "You got to drive, though."

We finished the beers we had and then we drove into Litch-field in Victor's Chevy. We must have looked like quite the pair, the long-haired heavyset old man, and the thin Portuguese boy. In the car, Terrence smelled funky, like cigarettes and beer, but like the woods too, perhaps like the mushrooms he harvested for money. I was glad he was getting me the beer, but I think I was even happier to get some separation between us. We could split up when we got back. We could split up and I wouldn't have to answer any more of his questions about Hannah, and have to see through his eyes what he thought about her.

Terrence asked me to eat with him that night. He had a small cookstove and I didn't know how to say no and so we sat together and got drunk on beer and ate some cheap steak he fried up with onions in a cast-iron skillet. He made some potatoes out of a box too and it was lousy food but it tasted sort of good after all the fast food I had been eating.

Afterwards we sat in the lawn chairs and it was a clear and beautiful night though the wind that came through the trees held some of the winter to come. I put on my coat but it still made me shiver. All that beer had completely gone to my head too and this might have contributed to the cold I was feeling. Terrence and I talked about fishing for a while, and then he told more about his life. How he chased the good weather, moving south when winter started to come.

"Anywhere there are woods, there are mushrooms," he said.

He spent his summers in the Northeast and in the winter he generally went down to the Carolinas. He camped the whole time and he worked when he wanted and it sounded like a decent life to me.

When we had exhausted that conversation we sat for a time in silence and smoked and kept our thoughts to ourselves. I was thinking of Hannah, of where she was, and whether or not tomorrow might be the day I would see her. On my morning drives past the school I kept expecting to just see her in front of one of those buildings, helping her mother unload a station wagon with all her things. Of course, I wouldn't be able to approach her just yet. I would need to give it some time, to pick my spot. I had no idea how she would react. And that was what was going through my mind when Terrence said, "How long they been looking for you?"

"Who?"

"The cops."

"What are you talking about?"

Terrence leaned forward in his chair and he brought his cigarette up to his lips and in the dark I sensed his eyes on my face, though I kept looking straight ahead, toward my campsite, to where the brook ran through the trees. "I been around a long time, boy," Terrence said. "I can tell when a man's running from something. You don't even have as much as a tent. Sleeping on the ground in the woods."

"Nah," I said. "I just don't have a tent."

"How long?" Terrence said. "Listen, I got no love for cops."

I leaned back and sipped from the can of beer. I didn't feel like lying. "Four days," I said.

"'Cause of what you did to the girl?"

"I didn't do anything to the girl."

"They know you're here?"

I shook my head. "I don't think so."

"What they want you for?"

"An accident."

"An accident?" Terrence said. "Cops never want people for accidents."

"A man died."

"How?"

"I don't want to talk about this," I said.

"Just tell me how and I'll let you alone."

"My buddy and I were robbing a house on Cross Island. Not even robbing it really, though it doesn't matter. We thought it was empty. It wasn't."

Terrence nodded. "Sounds like a bitch."

"It was," I said.

"Tell me one more thing," he said.

"What?"

"What's the girl got to do with it?"

I sighed. "It was her father."

"What you going to do to her?"

I looked over at him. "I'm not going to do a thing to her. I love her."

"There's a lot to this then," said Terrence.

I lighted a cigarette. "Tell me about it," I said.

We didn't say much more that night. We sat in the dark for a time and finished our cigarettes. Above us the tall pines shook with the autumnal breeze.

The next morning I woke to the drizzle of rain and I had a hangover. I stood up and opened the door to the car and for a few minutes I sat in the driver's seat with the door open and watched the soft rain fall. Terrence's trailer was there but his truck was gone. He must be in the woods.

I drove over the rolling hills to Litchfield and at the drive-through picked up a coffee and a sandwich. The day was cloudy and gray and the rain now was just a misting on the windshield. I came back down 75 and as I went I wished Victor's radio worked. It would be nice to listen to the radio. I passed the white sign that said WELCOME TO LINCOLN and then I was coming on the school when I saw all the cars. My heart flipped in my chest. This was the day.

I slowed down coming past the school, and everywhere, on both sides of the road, expensive cars were being unloaded by well-dressed men and women with their daughters. Bags and bags, clothes on hangers. I drove as slow as I dared and I scanned the people as I went but to tell you the truth, their faces were all blank to me. I was looking for Hannah and for Hannah only. Where was she? It seemed as if everyone had arrived at once, and I did not see her among them. I was almost past the school, and about to turn around and make another pass, when I saw the cars. Three of them, all state police cars. Most ominously, one of them had the colors of Rhode Island. We were more than two hours from Rhode Island. They were parked in a row in a small parking lot next to a large white house with pillars on the front. One of the Connecticut cars and the Rhode Island car were both facing toward the main road. The other car, in between them, faced back toward the athletic fields. Through the glass I saw the shadows of the men who sat in them. I kept on driving and when I looked in my rearview, they had not pulled out. Either they had not seen me, or they did not know yet what they were looking for. Because one thing was crystal clear: They were here for me. I didn't know what they knew. Did they just think I might decide to come here? Or did they know from Victor that this was my plan?

But one other thing was beyond dispute that morning. Hannah was here, or was about to be here.

It took me a while, but I was able to figure out how to get back to the campsite by doing a great circle through a number of towns, ending up in Litchfield, and then making my way back.

I parked the car and for a time I sat on the hood and smoked and thought about what to do. The rain was so light that it felt cool and good on my skin. It felt like some kind of cure for my hangover.

If they thought I was here, it meant that they figured out that I had Victor's car. I'm sure they didn't think I walked here. Maybe I could have taken a bus. But I had to assume that the car was made and that they were looking for it. That I got lucky on my last pass. I couldn't drive the car in the daytime anymore.

The school was maybe three miles away. I knew the general direction, and it would be an easy walk on the roads to get there, but the same rule applied. If they were out looking for me, a Portuguese kid walking a winding country Connecticut road would be easy to pick out. No, the only move was to go overland. To pick my way through the woods. And hope that I didn't get lost.

I set off sometime after noon. I just plunged right in behind my campsite, forded the small brook by leaping from rock to rock, and then I was off among the trees. It was a young forest, a mix of birch and poplars growing close together, and the land rose up and down in small hills. It was beautifully green in here, though, and the cover was great enough that what rain there was did not reach me. It was hard work, this walk, as I had to make my way over brush and fallen logs, and now and again I took a break and sat down on a mossy stump and rested. Soon the woods grew more piney, and the trees were farther apart. The forest floor was covered with a soft blanket of pine needles and I moved more quickly.

Then coming down this long hill, I saw breaks in the trees in front of me and as I got closer I heard shouts, playful shouts, and I walked to the edge of the trees. In front of me I saw girls playing soccer. I was behind the school and these were the athletic fields. The field was maybe twenty yards away and I was in the dark trees and there was no way they could have seen me.

There were all kinds of girls. Blond girls and dark-haired girls. White girls and black girls. Girls with short hair and girls with ponytails that bounced on the back of their necks as they ran. I sat down against the base of a large tree and I watched them. I scanned their faces for Hannah but she was not among them. I would have seen her right away. My eyes would have gone to her. I couldn't picture her playing soccer anyway. There was something nice about the game, though. The misty rain had stopped and a splintered sun appeared from behind the clouds. The green grass shone with moisture. And there were all those girls in motion, their shouts and their cries, the thudding of their feet, the calling of each other's names, a blur of girls, moving as one.

Those woods became my friend. They wrapped that small campus like a blanket and for days I wandered through them like they were mine. I stood in their shadows and watched girls playing sports, walking to class, standing in small groups talking. I circled the whole place and there were only a few buildings out of the reach of my sight. I didn't see any cops. I also didn't see Hannah.

A few times I saw a girl at a distance that I thought was her, only to have the girl move close enough for me to realize I had been mistaken.

Emboldened by the darkness of night, I roamed the empty campus like I owned the place. There was one security guard, from what I could tell, and you could hear him coming from a mile away because he whistled when he did his rounds. I'd duck behind a building and wait until he had passed. I learned all the names of the buildings, especially the low brick ones near the soccer field that I took to be the dormitories. Spencer Hall. Fuller Hall. Salisbury Hall. Bradford Hall. They were two-floor square institutional buildings and I walked their lengths in the dark, hoping to see through one of the windows, to get a glimpse of my girl.

But these girls were scrupulous about keeping their shades drawn, and I never saw more than a passing glimpse of a figure between the edge of shade and the window. I was losing hope.

Coming back to the campsite after one of these missions, I emerged out of the dark woods to discover that Terrence had returned, and was on his lawn chair in front of his trailer. I didn't want anything to do with him, but he was drinking beer and I wanted one. If he thought it odd that I appeared seemingly out of nowhere, he didn't say anything. He motioned for me to sit down, and I did and he reached for his cooler and handed me a beer.

"How's your girl?" Terrence asked.

I shook my head. "Nothing."

"Haven't found her?"

I looked toward where I had come from, the dark woods behind the campsite. "No," I said.

"Why don't you just call?"

"I don't know that she'll talk to me."

Terrence seemed to be considering this. "How 'bout this?" he said.

I looked over at him. "What?"

"Pretend you're delivering something."

"Yeah, right."

"I'm serious, boy. It'll work."

I shook my head. "I don't have a uniform or anything."

"It don't matter. You don't actually have to deliver anything. You just need to find out where she lives, right?"

"Yeah," I said.

"So just go to the school there, pull up, find a couple of girls and ask them. Say 'I have a package for Miss-whatever-her-name-is and can you tell me where I can find her?' Bet they give it right up."

"That's not bad," I said, thinking it over.

"Hell no," said Terrence. "It's good, what it is. That shit'll work."

I was actually grateful and showed it. I raised my beer to him and we clinked bottles. "Thanks, Terrence," I said.

"Then you can do whatever it is you going to do to her," he said.

"I told you I'm not going to do anything to her."

Terrence drew on his cigarette and he looked away. "What you say, boy."

I braced at this. I felt an anger come over me and when I looked at him, he had turned back toward me and his old face framed by his gray hair had a smug look on it. I could have smashed it with the beer bottle in my fist, that's how I felt about it. I said, "I'm not going to tell you again about that."

"Whoa, boy, relax," said Terrence.

I lighted a cigarette, breathed in. "I'm okay."

"Good," Terrence said. "Have another beer."

I swallowed the last of what I had and took the new beer from him. I drank it quickly. I was thankful for the idea and for the beer but I wanted to be away from him. I wanted to hit my bedroll and shut my eyes against the day.

The next morning I drove to Litchfield under steely skies and at the pharmacy I bought cigarettes, a big padded envelope, and a pen. Back at the campsite I saw that Terrence had once again left and I sat on the hood of my car and I wrote Hannah's name on the envelope and below it I wrote, Miss Watson's School. The day was cool and breezy but I didn't mind. I was filled with anticipation for what I was about to do.

I hiked back through the woods and when I reached the clearing that was the soccer fields, I stopped and I waited. My heart was somewhere between my chest and my throat, to tell you the truth. There were no girls around and I figured they were in class. I waited until I heard the shrill of a bell and then I left the woods and boldly walked across the soccer field. I reached a pathway that cut between buildings and stood there, thinking that any minute the state police were going to come bounding toward me, telling me to put my arms in the air, to stay where I was. Instead I heard voices, girls' voices, and from between the buildings came a knot of girls, four of them, and when they approached me, I did my best to look lost. I saw them taking me in, my jeans and my workboots, my flannel shirt, and I pretended to study the empty package in my hands. When they reached me, I said, "Excuse me."

They stopped. Stared at me. I looked down at the envelope again. I gave it my best voice. "Can you tell me where I can find," and I paused and looked down once more. "Ms. Hannah Forbes. Where her room is?"

Behind them I saw more girls coming. No sign of any teachers, though. Or security. I did worry that any moment Hannah would come around one of the buildings and see me there. I had no idea how she would react.

The tall girl in front said, "Hannah's in Fuller."

Next to her, a small blond girl said, "All packages go to the mail room." She pointed to a low building to our left. "In there."

I ignored her. "Do you know her room number?"

The tall girl said, "I think she's in 104."

"No, it's 105," a girl in the back said.

"Yeah, 105," said a third girl.

"Great, thanks," I said. A few more girls passed us and I turned and started to walk away. I stopped and studied the envelope until the girls I had talked to had moved on and I could see their backs. Then I took a right over the soccer field. I kept walking and when I was over a rise, I broke into a run and didn't stop until I reached the safety of the woods.

That night was dark and without moon. The nights were darker here in the woods than they were at home, where the ocean, even on cloudy starless nights, seemed to hold some of the light of day. I ate a fast-food dinner and sat around the campsite wishing I had some beer. I was real jumpy and I chain-smoked and watched the night come on. The evening seemed to stretch on forever and when I took off through the woods, it was all I could do to keep myself from running.

I came onto the campus the way I always did now, across the soccer field and I ran in a half crouch crossing it, heading for the cluster of brick dormitories on the other side. I stopped behind a tree when I reached the pathways lined with streetlamps and I looked around. The place was deserted, as it always was at this time, the girls safely ensconced in their dorm rooms. No sign of the security guard. No sign of teachers. No cops. I ran across the small quadrangle and in between two of the dorms, stopping to rest with the brick of Fuller Hall, where Hannah was, behind my back.

Two floors of windows were next to me, most of them still lit. Behind one of them was Hannah. My challenge was to discover which one.

I could eliminate the second floor. Room 105. That had to be on the first floor. If odd numbers were on the right, and even on the left, it should be the third one in, I figured, a mere thirty feet or so from where I stood.

I went to this window and stood in front of it. The shade was drawn but on the left side there was a sliver of open space. I put my eyeball right to it and tried to look in. I saw a lamp on a desk and behind it I saw what looked like the metal headboard of a bed. But that was all I could see. I stepped away from the window. I thought about what I should do now. I couldn't just knock on it, since there was no way of knowing for certain that it was Hannah's room. I had only one bite of the apple, I figured. Behind me I heard a foot-fall, like someone stepping on a branch, and I froze where I was. I looked to my right and I saw the light of a flashlight. I went quickly to the side of the window and leaned my body as far as it would go into the brick. A beam of light danced across the space I occupied between the two dormitories. It flitted over my head and caught my boots in its light. Then it was gone and I heard whistling. The security guard doing his rounds.

I stayed put until I was comfortable he was long gone. Then I went back to the window and when I looked through this time, what I saw seized my heart. She was only inches from me, sepa-rated by glass. I could only see the tiniest piece of her where she leaned over the desk, her bangs hanging over her forehead, a swipe of her face. There was only one thing to do. I didn't care what happened.

I rapped softly on the glass with my knuckles. Once and then again. A hand appeared at the bottom and the shade went up. Instinctively, I stepped back.

Standing there in the glass, staring out into the dark at me, stood Hannah. She wore a white tank top and pajama bottoms. Hannah slid the window up and when she did, I started to cry. I hadn't planned to but it just happened. Big, choking tears too. For a moment she just looked at me. She seemed too stunned to say anything and I was crying too hard to talk. It was like something opened inside me and I had no idea how to stuff it back in.

Hannah said, "I'm going to get the cops."

Suddenly I managed to talk. I said, "Don't do that, Hannah. Don't. Please. Don't. I just need to talk to you. Please. And then if you want, I'll go away. You can call the cops. Never see me again."

"You killed him," she said. "They said you killed him."

"No," I said, "you have to listen to me. Can we just talk, please? Please," I said. "Come with me. Ten minutes. Hear me and then you can go."

I wiped tears away from my face with the back of my sleeve and for a moment she didn't do anything. She just looked at me. Behind her the door opened and another girl came in the room. She was tall and blond and wore pajamas too. She looked frightened when she saw me standing there. But of course she wouldn't understand.

"Hannah," she said. "Is this him?"

"Come with me, Hannah," I said, and I reached for her hands. She didn't resist me. I helped her out and through the window.

"Can I just get a sweater?" Hannah said, when she stood next to me.

"Sure," I said.

"Emma, hand me a sweater and some jeans. My sneakers."

"Are you crazy?" Emma said. "You're going to get expelled."

"Just do it, Emma."

The tall girl went to the closet and came back with a pair of jeans, a bulky wool sweater, and a pair of white sneakers. She handed them out the window. Hannah dropped her pajama bottoms and in the dark I saw her beautiful legs where they came out of her panties. She wriggled into the jeans and then slid the sneakers on. She pulled the sweater over her head.

"What should I do?" the other girl asked.

"Just wait," Hannah whispered. "I'll be right back."

"This way," I said.

I led her in the dark through the campus I knew as well as she did, toward the soccer field.

We sat cross-legged on the dewy grass facing each other. Our knees touched. I tried to hold her hands but she would not let me yet. It was so dark I could barely see her face. I was grateful for the dark, because I wanted her to focus on my words, not my eyes or my mouth. I wanted Hannah to hear everything I had to say. I wanted the words to sit still in the air for her to gather in herself when she wanted to.

I spoke softly but insistently. I told her everything. I left nothing out. I told her all that had happened before she found me on the beach. I said how Victor had been at her grandmother's wake, and had gotten bad information that she had lived alone and that the house would be empty. How he saw the money under the carpet and that was why we had gone there. Because we were poor and it was a lot of money. We never would have gone into the house if we knew someone was there. I said that when she appeared on the stairs I could not stop looking at her. That I knew then that I loved her and I know that sounds crazy but that was the way it was. And how I never saw

her father until he was on me, until he drove me into the railing. I had only tried to get away from him. I didn't fight back
or do anything. He fell, I said. It was an accident and if I could
do anything to bring him back, I would. I said I wished that I
was the one who had gone over the railing. Only if I had I never
would have known her. We would not have had that time on the
island. And I could only speak for myself, but before then I had
been drifting through life without ever feeling anything, really
feeling anything, like I was one of those people who couldn't
experience pain, so that they could touch a hot stove and burn
the shit out of themselves and not know it.

When I was done, I stopped talking and I listened to her
breathe across from me. I was quiet. She cried. I wanted to reach
out to her but I was on her schedule. I let her cry and I cried
again myself. A brisk wind moved across the field and I felt it
on my shirt. I wanted her to tell me I had said enough. I wanted
her to tell me we were okay. I wanted to hold her. I wanted to lie
down next to her. I wanted to trace her face with my fingers.

Finally, she spoke. Barely a whisper. She said, "I believe you."

I whispered back, "Say my name."

"Why?"

"Please, I need to hear you say it."

"Anthony," Hannah said.

I put my hands on her arms. I slid them up near her shoulders. Sitting cross-legged like we were, we formed a wheel. I
leaned my head forward as far as I could.

"Come here," I said. She moved her face toward mine in
the dark. I turned my head sideways and sitting there in that
field our cheeks touched and when I pushed them closer together it hurt but neither of us cared at all.

Dr. Mitchell has taken a keen interest in my writing. He always asks me what I am working on, as if there is any question. He wants me to share it with him but I put him off, telling him I'm not ready.

"Your only allegiance is to the truth, Anthony," he says.

I feel like saying, tell me something I don't know. But I don't. What would be the point? We've had these arguments before, arguments about truth. Dr. Mitchell thinks that all truth is absolute, that something is either true or it isn't. I tell him that it would be nice if the world were that easy, but I know that it isn't. Truth is often a matter of perspective. I may see things differently from where I stand, than he does from where he stands. It doesn't make my views and understanding of things any less valid. It just makes them different.

Berta came to visit with news of Victor. Victor has not been to see me since I first came here, and I don't blame him. He has a hard time with it and has chosen to stay away. Victor has done well for himself. He married Maria, sweet-eyed Maria, who worked as a maid in that Cross Island mansion. When I first heard that, I thought it was really funny. Ironic even. It was almost as if we all had to pass through that house, like some kind of sacrament, before we could get on with the rest of our lives. The two of them have three children, Berta tells me, two girls and a boy. Victor has his own business doing plumbing and it keeps growing. There are these black box trucks all over town that say PEREZ PLUMBING AND HEATING on the side. He has something like ten people who work for him.

Berta says he and Maria bought a ranch house on the water on Great Island. From his windows he can see the Galilee harbor and the boats going in and out. He has a big grassy lawn that on nice days the kids run around on. There's a swing set. He has a spare tire around the middle and still has that mustache that he likes to comb. If I were there, I'd give him shit about it, you can bet on that. But I'll also admit that when Berta tells me all this, it makes me wistful. I mean that sometimes I still imagine that kind of life. A pretty wife and well-behaved kids and a nice house. Ball games on the weekend, backyard cookouts. Church on Sundays. Putting up a Christmas tree.

But I also know it's hard to have that life and also have the truth. There's a kind of willful ignorance that goes with living that way. You have to turn your back on the things that really drive you. The passion. And the desire. That electric feeling you get from going after what you really want. You have to live a lie. No one would admit that. Not even Victor. But I bet sometimes he feels it. Maybe when his whole house is sleeping, his wife and kids, and the neighborhood is quiet. Maybe he sits in a lawn chair in the garage with the door up and sneaks the cigarette he's no longer allowed to have. He looks out across the water to the lights of the boats leaving the harbor. And he taps that part of himself that is still alive, somewhere deep within, and he wonders what could have been.

In the dark I knocked on the door to Terrence's trailer. There were no lights on but his truck was parked near the trees. I heard him in there, knocking around and then the door opened and he stood in front of me wearing only his boxer shorts. He was lit from behind and I saw his massive stomach, his chest covered with gray hairs, and a scar that ran down his side like a seam. He peered behind me.

"Is that her?" he said.

"Yes," I said.

He stepped away from the trailer. "Let me get a better look at her," he said.

"Don't bother," I said but Hannah stepped forward until she was only five feet behind me. Terrence whistled through his front teeth.

"Damn," he said.

"Leave it alone," I said but he was looking over my head at her.

"Why else you get me at this time?" Terrence asked.

"I need your truck."

He laughed. "What do you mean, my truck?"

We both looked over at it. An old Ford, once red, now more rusty than anything. "They know the car."

"So? That's not my problem. I need my truck. How you think I haul this thing around?" He reached behind him to tap on the metal of the trailer.

"I'm taking the truck," I said.

"I tell you what," said Terrence. "Maybe you give me a piece ..." He nodded to Hannah. "And we can talk about it, okay?"

I pushed him so hard and so fast he had no time to react. It took him right off his feet and he fell backward and smacked his head against the side of the trailer. "Aw, fuck," he said, "my head."

I hated to do it but I had no choice. I rushed past him and into the trailer and there was only the one light but I scanned all the surfaces and there, on the small stove, I saw the keys. I went to them and I grabbed them and when I turned around, Terrence was blocking my way. His hair was all wild around his neck. He said, "You little shit."

His pudgy hands reached for me but I dodged them and then ran right into him. When we collided, I swung wildly at his face. My fist hit bone and I felt his hand crashing into the back of my head. I kept punching at him, as hard as I could. I had my eyes closed so the only way I knew I had hit him was the pain in my hand. I must have hit him ten times. He slumped to the floor. I heard him breathing heavy but he did not say anything. I didn't look down at him. I wanted no part of his face. I climbed over him and out into the campsite.

I didn't see Hannah right away. Then I heard her, on the other side of Victor's car, entering the woods. I found her at the edge of the brook and took her hand and led her back. Her eyes were wide and her hands were sweaty. She shook a little. I knew this was a lot for her at once and so I stopped and I hugged her. She hugged me back and in her arms I felt her return my love. "It's okay," I said. "This is going to get easier."

I picked up my oilskin bag and we went for Terrence's truck. Before we got in, I took Victor's keys and flung them as far as I could into the woods. The last thing we needed was Terrence trying to follow us.

We climbed into the truck and the upholstery was torn and the cab reeked of stale cigarettes. A milk crate on the passenger side floor overflowed with mushrooms. But it started right up and Hannah moved close to me on the bench seat and I steered us through the pine trees and out of the campground.

I just drove. I had no plan and no destination. I took a right turn in Litchfield and just followed the country highway in the dark. The old truck took us up and over hills and through black woods and past darkened houses. The night was cool but I kept my window rolled down so I could smoke. Hannah fell asleep shortly after we left, her face pushed into my right shoulder, one hand draped lazily across my thigh. Now and again I looked at her. At her beautiful sleeping face, the soft eyelids. It made me so happy to have her back that sometimes my hands left the wheel like some kind of spasm, the feeling threatening to spill out of me. I didn't know what direction we were going. It didn't matter. The only sense I had was of the curvature of the earth, us crawling along its spine.

I knew we were heading north when we crossed into Massachusetts. I had figured we would go west, to California maybe, but suddenly north felt right. Maybe we'd go to Canada, cross into another country. Truly begin anew.

Meanwhile Hannah slept on. She slept so well. The cool night came into the cab and she moved closer to me against it and I smoked with one arm out the window. We had the road to ourselves. There were the headlights moving across the trees and over the crest of hills. Hannah's easy breath of sleep. The nutty taste of tobacco in my mouth. I was not the least bit tired. I thought that as long as there was night, I could drive.

Sometime before dawn, the first blue light visible to the east, we crossed into Vermont. The woods were dense here and right to the edge of the road. The night began to lift and we followed a rocky stream. We went through small New England villages and then back into a forest. I passed a sign that said COZY CORNER CABINS and underneath it, VACANCY. I pulled into a turnoff and Hannah woke when I did and she said, "Where are we?"

"I think I found a place," I said, turning the truck around.

The office was a log cabin, someone's home. I knocked on the door and it took a while but a tall bearded man finally answered. He was still tugging on a pair of jeans and his flannel shirt was unbuttoned, his hairless chest at eye level and as white as paper.

"I saw vacancy on the sign," I said.

He looked me up and down. It had to be five in the morning but if he thought anything of this, he either didn't care or chose not to say anything. "Thirty-five bucks a night," he said, starting to button his shirt. "No maid service."

"Cash okay?" I said.

"Cash is king," he said.

I took bills out of my pocket and peeled off three twenties and a ten. "That's for two nights," I said.

He got me the key and stepped out onto the porch and pointed back into the woods to where I was to go. I saw him take in the old truck and Hannah in it, awake now, staring up at us.

The cabin was not much to speak of. There were six of them, identical, and in a row, with great pines looming over them like sentinels. In the early-morning light they looked like they had been dropped there, on top of the pine needles, almost as if they were for sale. They were shingled and had tiny front porches, not really serviceable, with just an overhang to keep you from the elements. There were no other cars in front of them.

Hannah and I walked like dead people. I was so tired. I looped my bag over my shoulder and we climbed out of the truck and up the one step and I keyed the door and stepped into the room. I flicked on the light and it was grim, a sad bed in the artificial overhead light, the musty odor of mothballs, a carpet with a deep pattern that you couldn't tell where the stains stopped and the checks started. Hannah went for the bathroom and I flopped right onto the bed.

With the shades drawn there was no telling if it was night or day. I don't remember Hannah killing the light. I slept like I had never slept before, without dreams, and the only thing I remember is her lying next to me, the rough feel of the comforter against my skin, and the smell of Hannah, that beautiful smell, her soap and her sweat, this girl that I had already given my life up for.

I woke in a near panic. I looked around. Hannah was on the edge of the bed. She looked back at me and in her look I saw the guilt and then I saw the phone in her hand.

"What did you do?" I said.

"Nothing," she said.

"Did you call somebody?"

"No," she said softly.

"Did you?"

"No," she said again.

"They won't understand," I said.

"I know."

"Then why?"

"I'm scared, that's all," she said, and the look on her face was so vulnerable, I wanted to take her lovely face in my hands and hold it, feel her pulse beneath my fingers.

I said, "I would never hurt you."

"I know."

"Come here," I said, and she did, she fell down next to me and I rolled toward her. I slung my arm across her belly and afternoon light slanted through the break in the heavy curtains. Narrow bars of gold on the thick carpet.

"I love you," I said.

She turned her face to me. "Do you?"

Her green eyes were wet. "Yes," I said.

"Okay," she said.

"Do you love me?"

Hannah's eyes flickered from the top of my head down to my waist. She was so shy sometimes it killed me. "I do love you," she said.

I undressed her slowly, as if each part of her was a mystery to be revealed. When she was naked on the bed, I spent the longest time just running my hands over all of her, from her toes to her feet, up her shapely legs and across the flat table of her belly, the rise of her breasts, to the soft whiteness of her bare throat.

There was a fury to our lovemaking that afternoon. We crashed together like we could not get enough of each other. Like we were trying to make up for the hours and the days we were apart.

When we finally collapsed, we lay side by side in the sweet quiet and we did not say anything. There was the rise and fall of our collected breath on the bed, the smell of the musty room, the smell of our sex. The alarm clock on the table next to us flipped a new number over, a flapping sound. Time was beating on. Not that it mattered. Inside that space, there was only Hannah and there was only me. No light, no moon, no night. The world didn't make it past those heavy drapes.

We were not perfect parents. What I would give to do things differently! You have no idea. Jacob was busy with his work, the company, and it's no secret that I started to drink. I know now that I am sober—I have this to thank for that, sometimes even flowers grow out of ashes—that I was depressed. At the time, I just thought I was bored. In that big house all day with nothing to do, Jacob at work and Hannah at school. I would close those heavy blinds and drink vodka on ice and watch bad television. I thought it was a temporary thing. Something to help me through a difficult time in my marriage. But it lasted ten years. It got so bad I had bottles of Smirnoff hidden all around the house. Under the couch. In the bathroom. Even in the tire well of the station wagon. The greatest guilt I have is how much my drinking cost me time with my girl. Jacob and I had been done for a while. We made a good show of it during Hannah's school year, though he worked as much as he did because he did not want to be home with me. And then in the summers he disappeared to the island and took Hannah with him. She got that from him, her love of the ocean. Unless it was a beautiful day, the island made me sad. It seemed so lonely out there on the point, nothing but fog and water. I was happy to have them gone, to be completely honest. I didn't have to hide my drinking in the summer. They were gone, and I could be myself in that big house. Even after Jacob died, I couldn't get myself to go there. Who knows how different things would have been? Would you have come for her if I was there? Would you two have even met?

Oh, but Hannah loved it there. She loved the rocky coast and she loved the beaches. She loved to lie in the sun and brown. I was always telling her she had to be careful, that the sun will age you if you're not careful. But she didn't care. She liked being alone in that old house. And I never worried about her. When you grow up with parents like us, you grow up quickly. You learn how to travel. How to be in society. What is expected of you. And you also learn how to be on your own at a young age.

We made love until we could not make love anymore. Until our very bones ached from coming together. I found a small town nearby and fetched us sandwiches and we ate on the bed, lying on our stomachs. I stood on that tiny porch and looked at the huge pines and out to the rural highway and I smoked. It was the only time I allowed myself away from her. But then I was back inside and in the dark of that room I watched Hannah sleep. I lay on my back and traced the spider-web cracks on the ceiling. And when the sadness rolled over me, it took me by surprise. Didn't I have everything I wanted? Wasn't she all I wanted?

Of course, there was all that we knew that went unsaid. In Rhode Island and in the western corner of Connecticut, we both knew they were looking for us. Men and women we did not know, and some that we did, whose entire existence right now was built around finding the two of us and tearing us apart. Taking Hannah away from me. Sometimes lying there, I pictured them. Cops and detectives, in some windowless room, map on the wall, going over different scenarios. Did they go to New York to try to vanish into the big city? Or had they

driven out west? Were they still in Connecticut, maybe at another campground?

And I'll admit that part of me liked their attention, how it
elevated the thing between me and Hannah, even though I was
afraid of what they wanted to do to us.

There was something else important that went unsaid. For
the first time in my life, I was away from the ocean. I know that
sounds silly, but the more we moved inland, into these forested
hills, the more I felt its absence. The ocean that was a different color every single day. The ocean that had given me work,
had given my father work. The ocean that when I rode on its
surface I was aware of its awesome strength and its power, at the
same time knowing that I was one of the few who knew how to
respect and love it. Not tame it because no man could do that.
I had been born to the sea. It was in my blood. It was all I had
ever known. And it saddened me to think that it might be gone
forever.

That second morning at the cabin, we opened the door to
cloudy skies and a cool, rawboned day. It looked like rain when
I stopped at the log cabin and dropped the keys in a wooden
box there for this purpose. Out on the rural highway, Hannah
turned to me in the cab.

"Anthony," she said.

"Yeah?"

"I need clothes."

I looked at her and I felt so stupid and selfish. She had come
directly with me that night at her school, and had not packed a
bag. She had on the same jeans and T-shirt and sweater she had
that night. "I'm so sorry," I said. "I completely spaced."

"And you need to do laundry."

"I do?"

She nodded. "Your clothes stink."

I lifted the front of my shirt up to my nose and smelled it. Sweat and cigarettes. "You're right," I said.

We continued to drive north through beautiful country. We were following a meandering brook that disappeared from the road before bending back alongside it. The heavy pine forest came right to the edge of the road and now and again when we came up a hill, we could see blue mountains in the distance.

Outside of Rutland the rain came, and it fell so hard the shoddy wipers on the truck could barely keep it off the glass. We got burgers at a drive-through and then we pulled into the parking lot of a giant strip mall. I pointed. "Wal-Mart," I said. "We'll get you clothes there."

Hannah looked at me. "Are you serious?"

I shrugged. "Got a better idea?"

We held hands and walked through the wide aisles of the store like some married couple. She was used to shopping in fancy stores in Boston, but she didn't even have a wallet, and the only money we had was the cash that I took from under the carpet that night. This was not a time to be picky. And Hannah, to her credit, managed to give in to it, and while I waited she modeled things for me, a pair of jeans that fit her like a glove, a white button-down shirt, and a sundress that I loved, blue and white checked, and short enough that when she moved its bottom hem swayed and showed off all of her lovely tanned legs. We bought her two sweaters and a coat, underwear and socks. We filled a cart with clothes. And when we pushed the cart out to the truck in the rain, her arm was looped in mine, and I knew that this may not be what she was accustomed to, but that on some level she was grateful.

Farther down the same strip, we found a Laundromat and I

brought my bag inside and got change out of the machine. The place was empty, other than the old woman who ran it, sitting on a folding chair watching a soap opera on a small black-and-white television. All my stuff fit into one of the big washers and Hannah and I sat down in the middle of a row of molded plastic seats to wait for it.

Hannah leaned into me and she rested her head on my shoulder. She was bored. "We'll be out of here soon," I said.

"Then what?"

"I don't know," I said, and I didn't. Next to me on the seat was a stack of magazines and I picked up the one on the top. *Vermont Life,* it was called. I flipped it over and on the back was a picture of these new homes on top of a mountain. In the picture they were surrounded by snow and they looked quite beautiful. A-frames with big windows. Tall pine trees around them and you could see where the land dropped off and there was a hint of broad valley behind them. They were winter houses for rich people, the kind of people Hannah had known her whole life. The kind of person Hannah was when she wasn't with me. I pointed at the picture. "How about here?" I said.

Hannah looked down at it. "Stratton Mountain," she said, reading from the caption.

"What do you think?" I said. "We'll go there and get ourselves one of these houses. Live on top of a mountain. Learn how to ski or something. Wake up every morning and look across the valley."

"You're crazy," she said.

I stood up. "Excuse me," I said to the old lady watching her soap. She turned in her seat and looked at me. I held up the magazine to her and she was too far to see it real good but she peered at it anyway. "Do you know where this is? Stratton Mountain?"

She turned back to her show. "About half hour south," she said.

"We must have passed it."

She didn't look back at me. "Depends what way you came."

I didn't answer the old woman. I sat back down and I smiled at Hannah. I nudged her with my elbow. "We'll get one of these houses," I said. She rolled her eyes at me and I loved her for it.

On the road heading south, we crested a hill and something happened that I had only seen in the middle of the North Atlantic. The sun cracked through the clouds and it shone brightly on the front of the truck while the bed behind was pounded with heavy rain. Two worlds in a matter of inches.

At a gas station I filled up and then I left Hannah in the truck and I went into the phone booth. After I dialed, the machine came on and told me I owed a dollar seventy-five and I pumped the quarters into it. A click and then it was ringing. Berta answered on the third ring.

"Hello, Mama," I said.

She spoke to me in Portuguese. Either someone was there or she knew they had tapped the lines. She told me to come home, to turn myself in. It was the only way out of this mess, she said.

"I can't do that," I said. "This is my life. I'm living it."

"You're sick," she said to me, practically spitting the words at me over the phone.

"I have to go," I told her, aware that I had already been on too long. I had seen the movies. No doubt there were men in a van in front of my house running a trace on this very call, trying to narrow in on this roadside spot in Vermont. "I love you, Mama," I said, and then I hung up.

For a while as we drove, her voice echoed in my head and it made me sad to hear it. Berta didn't deserve any of this, I knew that. She only wanted good things for me, she only wanted me to be a good man, like her husband, my father, had been. She didn't understand the things that drove me, and she may have loved like this once, but it had been a long time. It was too much to expect her to understand.

Soon the road began to climb and we were into the mountains, coming around turns to see valleys and rolling hills opening up before us. The pine forest had given way to oaks, birch, and maples, and in the now steady afternoon sunlight, some of them showed the first red of fall. It was beautiful. My spirits lifted to see it and I put my hand on Hannah's thigh and I squeezed.

We came onto Stratton Mountain just as the light was failing. There wasn't much to it. More of a big hill, with a ski lift you could see cutting up either side of it. Some restaurants and a few hotels. Lots of condos. We drove past all of it and when we were coming down the other side, I saw a green sign that said, Mountainside homes. Underneath it said, starting at $500,000. I smiled at Hannah. "This is us," I said.

She shook her head. "What are you going to do?"

"I'll show you."

We drove up an unpaved tree-lined road and when we reached the top, the land leveled and there were no trees. The sun had fallen behind the distant hills but in the last of the light we could see for miles. Foothills and ridges leading to where we were. There were all these houses up here and all of them were dark. The A-frames from the pictures, chalets with big porches that looked down over the mountain. Not one of them had a car in front of it. They were new enough that there was no yard to speak of around them. Just dirt piled here and there. I stopped in front of one and got out and climbed up the porch and looked through the sliding glass doors into the house. It was hard to see in the light, but I saw that it was empty.

"What do you see?" Hannah called up to me.

"It's empty," I said. "Let's try another."

We tried two more and they were also bare inside. But the third one I looked into, slightly back from the road, had what appeared to be furniture. I looked around the doors and the windows for signs of some alarm. But I didn't see anything, and I told Hannah to wait out front and I walked around the back. There was wood stacked underneath another porch and next to it was a door. I tried it and it was locked. I picked up a big square piece of the firewood and I stepped back. I threw it at the window on the door and it went right through, almost cleanly, it seemed, the glass falling to the floor inside. I reached through and unlocked the door.

I was in a basement. In the dark I made out a wooden staircase and I went to this and climbed the stairs. I opened the door and I was in a great room, and in front of me were the sliding glass doors that led to the high porch in the front. I felt around the wall for a light switch and I found one, and when I clicked it the room flooded with light. The ceiling had to have been forty feet high. There was a stone fireplace against one wall, and a stone chimney that went all the way to the ceiling. Leather furniture and bookcases filled with books and board games. A big kitchen and a staircase that led to a second-floor balcony that looked over the room.

I went to the sliding doors and unlocked them and stepped out.

"Come on," I said to Hannah, who stood outside the truck now.

"It's someone's house," Hannah said.

"No one's here," I said.

She looked reluctant but she came up the stairs. The first thing I did was look in the fridge. It was empty save for a couple of bottles of champagne and fifteen or so bottles of beer. The freezer was full of frozen meat. Steaks and whole chickens and all kinds of things I didn't recognize. This was better than I thought.

Hannah said, "What if they come back?"

"They won't," I said. "Not for a while."

"How do you know?"

"There's no snow," I said. "That's what they come here for, right? Snow?"

I parked the truck around back, in the dirt yard, where it couldn't be seen from the road. While I was at it, I brought a handful of the cordwood upstairs and I built us a fire in that huge fireplace. I closed the heavy drapes in front of the slid-ing glass doors and we only used one light in the kitchen and a standing one in the living room. No reason to take any chances. I took two big steaks out of the freezer and put them in a pan of water to thaw.

"Have a beer," I said to Hannah where she sat on one of the overstuffed leather chairs in front of the fire.

"I don't want a beer."

I smiled. "Champagne it is then."

I held one of the bottles over the sink and took off the wrapping and then twisted the cork until it popped. A little of the champagne cascaded out. There were wineglasses in one of the cupboards and I filled two of the glasses and brought one over to Hannah. I sat down in the chair next to her. The fire was going good and it kicked orange-and-red shadows around the room. I reached my glass to Hannah's and we clinked the two of them together.

"Make a toast," I said.

"To what?"

"I don't know. To us. Something."

"To us," Hannah said, and I raised my glass and she did, too, and we drank.

I said, "I bet they have a bathtub."

"So?"

"You could take a bath."

"You want me to take a bath."

"No," I said, "I just thought you'd like it, that's all. When these steaks thaw, I'll cook them up. You must be hungry."

"Okay," she said, and she stood and left me, climbed the stairs. She walked with the lifelessness of the exhausted. I didn't blame her, it had been a hard couple of days.

A few minutes later, I heard water running through the pipes. I lighted a cigarette and looked at the fire. It was a real good fire. Yellow-and-red flames rising above the burning wood. That great fire smell spilling out into the room. I stared up to the balcony where Hannah was. I looked around this great room. The high ceilings and the leather furniture. The rectangular windows up high that the moonlight slanted through.

I ashed my cigarette into a large painted vase next to my chair. My arms, running along the supple leather of the chair, were suddenly heavy. Not that it mattered. I had everything I had ever longed for. I remember thinking that there was nothing else I needed.

fried the steaks in a cast-iron pan and pretty much smoked out the whole kitchen. I ran around opening windows until it cleared out some. We ate the steaks with salt and pepper in front of the fire. Hannah wore only a tank top and her underwear. Her skin was flushed pink from the hot bath and her hair was still damp and stuck to her head. She was ravenous. I watched her eat her steak and when she was done she looked up at me with her big green eyes and in that look, I saw the little girl she once was. The mask of the years fell away and she was eight or nine, wanting to leave the dinner table. My heart went out to her. She seemed so vulnerable.

We slept that night in the master bedroom. We had a giant sleigh bed and with the windows open the cool mountain air came in. The comforter was down and soft and underneath it we locked our warm legs together. At one point I woke full of need and we made love silently and slowly, and afterward I kept my arms wrapped so tightly around Hannah that with my open mouth against her bare back I could taste the salt from her sweat.

In the morning we drove through bright sunshine out of

the new complex and down to the village to a general store and bought cigarettes and coffee, bread, eggs, and some loose potatoes. We didn't leave the house for three days. We laid around with the curtains drawn and played games. We played marathon games of Monopoly, and Hannah always won. She seemed to get the big properties right away and she always killed me. We drank the beer and the rest of the champagne. We ate scrambled eggs and toast for breakfast and every day I thawed something different from the freezer. Steaks, chicken, lamb chops. We took long baths together in the big tub, my arms wrapped under her arms, her hair in my face. We made love on the couch, on the living room floor, in the bathroom.

It was a lovely time, and I didn't want it to end.

We drank a lot of beer one night and when Hannah drank she often became sullen. This time she became almost euphoric, and at one point she stood and jumped onto the leather couch, and facing toward the fireplace, she began to dance. There was no music but it did not seem to matter. Her arms moved from her sides up to her hair. She would mess up her hair so that it streamed in front of her face, and she shook her slender hips, and she dipped her arms down to her toes and then up to the ceiling. She jumped up and down and she spun around. I sat cross-legged on the floor and I watched her. She moved with abandon. She moved without fear. I had wanted nothing more than to watch her let go, really let go, and now that she was, it was almost too much for me to handle. She danced to the beat in her head. She danced until she could not anymore. Then she ripped off her shirt and stood in front of me bare-breasted, her hair falling down and obscuring her eyes, her arms defiantly at her sides.

And in the middle of the night, we fought.

Hannah had been asleep for an hour or so but it wouldn't come for me. I lay next to her and I watched the pale moonlight stream through those high windows and I listened to her breath. I thought about home, about Galilee, and the cool air reminded me of the season, and that there were not many trips left for the swordfish fleet. If my life had not been turned upside down, I might have been on the North Atlantic that very moment, maybe on watch under the stars. Or maybe I would be sleeping on my bunk below, exhausted enough from a hard day's work to ignore the peaks and valleys of the ocean that we moved through. And I guess I knew then that I had given up a lot to chase this girl. And it's not that I had regrets, because I didn't. I made the decisions I made because they were the only decisions to make, and when I looked over at her sleeping face, I understood how right it was. Still, lying there in the dark mountains of Vermont, I longed for the life I had always had. For the simple clarity of the sea.

Next to me Hannah started to thrash around a little, dreaming. She was having a nightmare. I slid next to her and I reached for her hair and ran my hand through it.

"Hey," I said. "It's okay. Wake up. It's okay."

I meant to bring her to slowly, but I startled her. Her eyes full of fear and then she slapped me. Hard, right across the face.

"What the fuck?" I said.

"You scared me."

I wiped at my face. "You didn't have to hit me."

She rubbed her eyes and she looked away from me. She didn't say anything. I said, "Jesus, you could say you're sorry."

Hannah rolled over on her side. She said, "I want to go home."

And perhaps it was because while she slept I had been thinking my own thoughts of home, and of the sacrifices I had made for the two of us, that this angered me. I grabbed her roughly and tried to turn her back over, to face me. She resisted and I said, "Come here, look at me."

"I'm tired of looking at you," she said.

I got on top of her then, flipped her onto her back. She squirmed underneath me, and I used my knees to pin her arms down. "Look at me," I said, but she wouldn't. Her eyes roamed to the left and right but never up, never up at my face.

"You're hurting me," she said.

I gazed into her eyes then, those green eyes, and I saw the pain in them, the fear, and I had never wanted to frighten her and now I was and I hated myself for it. I lifted my knees off her arms. "I'm sorry," I said.

"Get off me," she said.

I moved off her and onto my back. We were side by side looking up at the wooden ceiling. "I didn't mean anything," I said.

"I just want to sleep," she said.

"You shouldn't have hit me," I said.

"You shouldn't have woken me like that. What was I supposed to do?"

"I don't want to fight," I said.

"Then let me sleep," she said. "Please? I just want to sleep."

"Okay," I said softly.

Hannah rolled back away from me. Outside I heard the wind moving across the mountains. There was a lot more I wanted to say. We had never had a fight before, not a real one, not like this. I didn't want anything to change between us. There was so much out in the world, beyond that bedroom, that was conspiring around the clock to keep us apart.

The thing that frustrates me the most, Anthony," Dr. Mitchell said to me last week, "is that we have never been close to a breakthrough. Do you know what I mean by a breakthrough?"

We were sitting in his office. Outside the big windows a cool autumn rain fell. I had been watching it fall, wondering if anyone's brain was fast enough that they could actually count each thread of rain. I hadn't been listening to Dr. Mitchell, though I heard this last part.

I nodded. "You mean that we've never come through something to stand on the other side."

He smiled. His teeth aren't very good for someone who smiles all the time. "Metaphorically, yes, Anthony, that's what I mean. More specifically, related to you, we've never reached a point where I can say, 'now he gets it.' Sometimes I think we should bring in someone else for you to see."

"But I like you, Dr. Mitchell."

"I like you, too, Anthony, but that's hardly the point. Look, you're very bright, we both know this. You are capable of sophisticated thought. You read all the time and now you are writing. Which I think you should share with me, by the way. But let me ask you something."

I looked past him again to the window. There is a giant oak right outside and its limbs spread out in all directions. For a moment it looked to me like an umbrella, with the rain spilling off it. "Go ahead," I said.

"Do you ever think of getting out of here, Anthony? Do you think about living on the outside again? With other people? Getting a job, being around friends and family?"

I crossed my legs. I stared at Dr. Mitchell, his wild hair. "I don't know," I said.

He leaned forward. "I don't believe you," he said.

"No?" I said.

"I don't," he said, shaking his head. "Here's what I think. I think you think about it constantly. I think that every time your mother comes here it breaks your heart. You want to be able to take care of her, Anthony. You see her getting older and wonder what will happen if she gets sick. Because somewhere inside you is someone who cares, who really cares. And you can't help her from in here."

I couldn't look at Dr. Mitchell anymore because I thought I was going to cry. This time I studied the books that line his walls. "You can read my story," I said.

"It's a story?"

"Yes. A true story," I said.

"I would appreciate that, Anthony," he said.

"I'm not finished yet, though."

He nodded. "I can wait. Here's the thing, Anthony. What I truly want you to understand. I want nothing more than to stand in front of that board and recommend to the state that you be released. I want that so badly for you. But I can't get there if we continue this long stalemate. Does that make sense?"

I gave him what he asked for. I was anxious to get back to my room, to my notebook and my seat with the view of the grounds and the hint of blue ocean in the distance. I wanted to get back to my thoughts.

I nodded. "It makes sense."

Dr. Mitchell smiled again. "Good," he said. "Good."

We lay in bed in that A-frame and I tried to count Hannah's freckles. We had been up for hours, waking to make love and then rolling around together, pretending to sleep, letting our hands move languidly over each other. She didn't know what I was doing at first, but then she saw me using my finger to count and she got mad.

"I want to know how many there are," I said.

"I hate them," she said. "Quit it."

I kept counting. "They're beautiful," I said.

She pushed my hand away from her face. "Quit it," she said.

"But they're beautiful."

"They're ugly, I hate them."

I grabbed her ribs then, above her waist, with both my hands and I tickled her. She squirmed and tried to escape but I had her good. "Say they're beautiful," I said.

She shrieked. "No," she said, "I won't."

I tickled her more, running my fingers across her sides. "Say they're beautiful," I said.

"Okay, okay, stop it and I will," she said.

"Say it," I said, not letting go.

"They're beautiful," she finally said. "Okay?"

I let her go. "Can I count them again?"

"No," she said, and she pretended to pout and it was about the most adorable thing I had ever seen.

Our fourth day in Stratton we got back in the truck and drove down the big hill to the general store where I had bought the supplies. Hannah sat close to me on the bench seat and there was no lingering residue from our fight. We had showered together and our hair was still wet. The day was warm and sun-splashed and you could not help but be happy because of it. I held her hand. Other drivers waved to us as we passed, which seemed to be a Vermont thing. We waved back. It was now September but it still felt like summer.

At the general store, Hannah stayed in the truck while I went inside. There were a few people inside, a couple talking down one aisle, an old man perusing the beer. I went to the back and got Hannah the chocolate milk she wanted, and myself a coffee, and I also picked up a couple of ready-made sandwiches they had in a case. Then I went to the counter and the man behind it, the same guy who had been there the other day, asked me if there was anything else I needed. He was very tall, with several days of growth on his chin, longish hair tucked under a baseball cap. I asked for cigarettes, and when he turned around to get them I looked down at the *Boston Globe* in front of him and what I saw on its front page made my stomach seize with fear. For there, on the left of the page, above the fold, were two photos side by side. The one on the left was of me, a picture I had taken for the fishing co-op, a head shot. My hair was a little longer then but it was a good likeness. Next to my photo was one of Hannah, a studio-type shot, taken for her yearbook, I guessed. It was a wonderful picture of her, even though it was in black-and-white. The lighting emphasized the cut and height of her cheekbones. Her full lips.

I must have been in such shock seeing those pictures that I almost forgot to peel my eyes away from the paper on the counter. The man was back and he put my cigarettes down and then he looked down at the paper to see what I was looking at. He looked back up at my face and then he peeked down again. I swear he recognized me. I almost wanted to run out of there but I knew enough to hold my ground.

"That's fifteen seventy-six," he said.

I took a twenty out of my pocket and handed it to him. My hands shook a little bit. "You want a bag?" he said, handing me my change.

"That'd be great," I said.

He reached below the counter and came up with a brown bag and snapped it open and quickly filled it.

"You have a good day now," he said.

It was all I could do not to run out of there. I climbed into the truck and placed the bag between Hannah and me and started the engine. As we drove out, I looked up toward the door of the general store, and I saw the clerk in the doorway staring at us going by. For all I knew he was writing down the license number. Maybe there would be a cop around the next corner.

I drove us back to the new development and I didn't say anything to Hannah about what I had seen. I don't know what I expected but I guess it never occurred to me that we would be big enough news to make the front page of the *Globe*. I pulled the truck all the way behind back so that it could not be seen at all from the road.

Inside I made sure all the drapes were drawn and the windows were closed. I turned off any of the lights we had left lit. Hannah sensed my tension, and she said, "What's going on?"

"We're going to have to leave," I said.

"When?"

"When it gets dark," I said.

I spent that entire day crouched in the front of the upstairs window while Hannah lay on the bed and played with her hair. Any minute I expected to see them come up the dirt road and by the new houses. In my mind I imagined a phalanx of cars and vans, state troopers and SWAT teams. The type of teams that descended on Tony Montana's house in *Scarface*.

In the end, though, it was one state trooper. I saw the black-and-green boxy car coming up the road, driving slowly past each house, looking at each one. It was crawling, maybe five or ten miles an hour. I closed the drapes until there was only a slit for me to see through. I turned to Hannah, and said, "Be really quiet."

"Why?"

"Just do it."

The trooper came to a halt in front of the nearest house to us, the only other one that I guessed had already been occupied. The door to the car opened and out stepped a tall dark-haired man with that square state trooper hat, the uniform with the jackboots, gun prominently on his hip. He walked slowly up to the door of the house and as I watched he knocked on it and he waited for a moment. He lowered his head and peered through the glass on the sides of the door. He shielded his eyes with his hands. Then he stood back up and started to walk back toward his car. Only he did not get in. He kept coming across the dirt road toward the house we were in.

I let go of the drapes and quickly joined Hannah on the bed.

"We have to be dead quiet," I whispered.

She went to speak but I put one hand over her mouth. "Shush," I said softly.

We lay there and we didn't move. The minutes ticked by, and then I heard a knock on the sliding glass doors below us, and Hannah stirred beneath my hand, and I knew it was because she had no idea what was going on, but I also knew she needed to trust me here. Another knock came and then silence. I figured he was looking in the window. Don't go around back, I prayed. If he went around back he would see the truck and he would see the broken window and the glass on the hard dirt and it would all be over.

Time opens up in situations like that. The air was pregnant with each silent beat of it. Any second I was prepared to hear footsteps coming up the basement stairs, perhaps the crack of a radio, or a deep man's voice telling us to come downstairs, keep our hands where he could see them.

But once again we dodged a bullet. I heard the engine of the police car start up and I left Hannah and crept across the carpet to the window. I parted the narrowest slit between the drapes and I gazed out. I saw him say something into the box he held in his hand and then he did a quick U-turn. He did not look back at the house, back at us. He drove quickly down the still-new road and disappeared below the hill.

We holed up in the house until dark. Then we climbed into the truck with all of our things and the last of the beer from the fridge. We drove slowly through the development and when we reached the main road, I took us past the ski village and out to the state highway. My nerves were frayed from the close call. I opened a beer and kept it between our legs. Hannah and I did not talk. I headed south, toward Massachusetts. The only plan I had was ill formed at best. The truth was, I wanted what Hannah wanted, to go home. I wanted to be back on familiar ground. There might be a hornet's nest there, but that was my coastline, my village, and I knew it as well as I knew the back of my hand. I thought that we could avoid whatever might be waiting for us. I thought that standing again on that spit of land might clear my head, allow me to figure out how we could be together. For the one thing that rose above all others was that. Hannah and me. Not letting them keep us apart.

The night was clear and bright with a full moon. It rose above the trees in front of us, massive and chalky white, its lakes silvery in the dark. At the Massachusetts border we stopped at a rest stop and ate our sandwiches. Then I peed in the woods and smoked leaning against the truck. I got back in and we stuck to back roads, moving through small towns and back out again, past marshy land and more woods. I didn't use the map. I drove the truck like it was a boat, pointing it south and just going.

After midnight we crossed into Connecticut. I found another state park and pulled into it. There was a reservoir here and the parking lot was deserted. I put the truck under the trees and we got out. I wanted a motel room but now that I knew we were in the *Globe*, I figured we were everywhere. Half of New England was probably looking for us. Motel clerks with my image memorized, just waiting for me to walk through their door so they could be a hero. Get their own names in the paper and on television.

We rolled my bedroll out on the wet grass next to the reservoir and in the moonlight its water was glassy and streaked with white. We bundled up against the first cold of autumn as best we could. We made furtive love, not bothering to take our clothes off, and afterwards Hannah cried and I told her it would all work out.

"There's nowhere for us to go," she said.

"I won't let them take you from me," I said.

"Promise me you won't do anything crazy."

"I'll take care of us," I said.

We fell asleep with our arms around each other, our faces inches apart, her bangs on my forehead.

A few hours later I woke and it was still dark, though the moon had set. The sky was a pale violet. I heard a loon out on the water. It was time to go.

I woke Hannah and she grumbled, and said, "Let me sleep."

"You can sleep in the truck."

And she did, she leaned against the far window and used a sweater as a blanket. I wanted to drive during the night. I didn't want to be out on those roads in broad daylight, where any cop could see us going by. No doubt they knew the truck. If not from finding Terrence, then from the clerk in Stratton.

I kept the window open and my elbow leaning out it. I opened another beer, just to get rid of the socks on my teeth. I liked the driving, the feeling of movement. That we were doing something.

The day arrived slowly. By dawn we had reached the coast, somewhere in Connecticut. The first of the sun spread across the water. I drove along an ocean road with big houses on one side and it warmed my heart to see the blue-green Atlantic, the birds diving over the rocks and the jetties.

In time we found a public beach and I pulled into its large parking lot. The sun was up now but it was still early. There were a handful of cars and I parked near them. Hannah was awake now, and she said, "Where are we?"

"The beach," I said.

We got out and walked across the parking lot to the sand. It was a long beach with a quiet stretch of ocean, the waves only small curled whitecaps coming into shore. A few people walked dogs and some others jogged on the harder sand near the water. I took Hannah's hand in my own and I imagined we looked like one of those older couples you see, still holding hands after forty years of marriage, going for long walks in the morning just to spend time together.

We didn't even know what day of the week it was. The beach filled up around us like some kind of time-lapse photograph. At first we were alone but by midmorning blankets were right next to blankets, umbrellas as far as you could see.

"It must be Saturday," I said to Hannah.

Not that we cared. The day was midsummer hot for September. Clear blue skies and no horizon. We slept in the hot sun with our warmed legs touching. We ran down to the water and charged into the ocean, splashing around, spraying each other like children. We kneeled in the shallow waves and let them roll over our shoulders. We kissed and tasted the salt water on each other's tongues. We walked into the parking lot and bought hot dogs and Cokes from a vendor for lunch. Then we slept some more.

We were like kids on vacation, young lovers home from college. I saw how others looked at us, our playfulness, and I knew they envied the intensity of our love. We wore it like clothes.

In the afternoon the beach emptied as it had filled, one family, one couple at a time. Soon we had most of our section to ourselves and by early evening, we were the only ones left who were not jogging or walking dogs. I recognized some of the same dog walkers from the morning and it was as if the day had been book-ended by their stroll.

We watched the sun fall out of the sky with Hannah sitting between my legs, my arms wrapped around her waist. I kept kissing the nape of her neck, where her soft hairs were. She tried to stop me, teasingly smacking at my hands. But I wasn't going to give in. I had no way of knowing how many days, how many hours, how many minutes, we had together. In front of us the sun had left the day and the sky was the rosiest of pinks. The air cooled around us. I pulled her back on top of me, and she tried to wriggle free, but I wouldn't let her go.

It's something to watch your little girl become a woman. It seemed to happen overnight. One day she's riding her bike in the driveway, skinning her knee, watching cartoons on Saturday morning. Then the next day boys are picking her up in cars. Hannah somehow seemed to leapfrog those awkward years most girls go through when they are teenagers. Her skin was always perfect. She never needed braces. She got tall without picking up bad habits, like stooping her shoulders when she was around boys. She moved with a grace that made other girls want to be like her. Want to be near her. She made friends easily but she was just as happy being by herself. Mostly, I admired the way she was around boys. She could take them or leave them. They didn't define who she was. She didn't spend all her time trying to please them at the expense of herself. God knows, plenty of grown women, myself included, have yet to figure that out.

It was her idea to go to Miss Watson's. I suppose we always knew she would go away to school. We gave her the option of some of the coeducational schools but she wasn't interested. I know Jacob was anxious to get her out of the house, away from me and my depression. He was right to do it, though things got worse for me while she was gone. The weekends she came home I did my best to clean myself up. I made sure the house was spotless. I resisted having a drink until the afternoon. I opened all the curtains and let the light in. I bought flowers and put them around. Jacob would come home early and the three of us would go out to dinner, like normal people. And it's funny, but Hannah was what kept us together. She was the light of Jacob's life, more important than anything, and I loved her very much, in my own way. It's different with mothers and daughters. It can be hard sometimes. But those nights when we had dinner, she would tell us all about school, about her friends, about her teachers, about dances they went to. She'd tell funny stories about her friends' parents, and it never occurred to us that her friends couldn't do the same thing to us because they had never met us. Hannah didn't bring them home and that makes me very sad now. She didn't want to bring someone into our house.

We crossed into Rhode Island after midnight. Driving along the coast in the dark, every set of headlights behind me made me nervous. Cars with roof racks outlined against the night might have been the roof lights of a squad car. The tranquility of the day had given way to the uncertainty of the darkness. I spent as much time staring into the rearview mirror as I did with my eyes on the road.

We came through Westerly and with the streetlights shining onto the road I saw that we were not being followed. I relaxed a little bit and brought Hannah close to me in the cab. It had been hours since we last spoke, though there was no tension between us. It was as if all that had needed to be said had been said, and now we were doing precisely what made sense. We were going home. As much as that was possible. Besides, we were both sun-weary from the day at the beach, a feeling that was both pleasant and exhausting at the same time. I could still feel the sand between my toes.

We came onto Route 1 and there was less traffic here, and I drove slowly, carefully obeying the speed limit. Soon we passed the giant water towers and the road became one-way toward the sea. We were the only vehicle. I rolled down my window and that familiar smell, of brine and of seafood, of marsh and of bay, came into the truck. It lifted my heart to smell it, and I reached over and squeezed Hannah's thigh.

"Almost there," I said.

She didn't respond.

I came through the old neighborhood the back way, past all those fishermen shanties, all of them dark at this hour. I killed the lights on the truck and we moved silently by the small houses with their fishing equipment piled in the yards and driveways. Sad little houses on concrete blocks.

I turned down the street that ran parallel to the one I had lived in with Berta. Halfway down it, I brought the truck along the curb and killed the engine.

"This will only be a minute," I said to Hannah.

I took her hand as we both climbed out my side of the truck. A few houses away a dog started to bark. I remembered the dog. A dark-colored pit that its owner kept on a short leash tied to a tree in his front yard. Beyond that, the neighborhood was quiet.

"This way," I said.

Holding hands, we crept between two dark houses. We walked on sandy earth, more sand than dirt. We came to a steel fence and a gate and I opened it and we stood facing the back of the house I grew up in. I brought Hannah right to the back of the house and we stood against the clapboards and I looked around the corner to the front and the street. I did not see any cars and the house itself had no lights on. This was what I expected.

The lock on one of the living-room windows that faced

the back had been broken for as long as I remembered and I pushed on the window and it gave way.

I whispered to Hannah, "Climb through and wait for me."

I looped my knuckles together to give her a boost and she stepped on them and then slid herself over the sill. I pulled myself up and slid over myself and we stood in my living room. It took a moment for my eyes to adjust but everything was exactly the same. There was the couch, and the rocking chair, the television, the painting of Madonna and child on the wall. Light from the streetlamps came through the front windows. It was enough to see by. I took Hannah's hand again and led her to the stairs.

We climbed them carefully and at the top we stood side by side, looking into the room where Berta slept. She had a night-light on in the outlet on the far wall and it spread a small amount of yellow light across the carpet and up the wall. My mother was on her back on the bed, and we could hear her soft snores.

We moved into the room and stood at the edge of her bed, looking down on her. She stirred slightly, as if sensing our presence, but then she continued to snore.

I leaned down and I kissed her on the forehead. I could make out her sweet wide face in the dark. I came up and looked at her again, and then I leaned down once again and kissed her wrinkled skin. Her eyes opened and I thought she might scream. I wouldn't have blamed her if she had. She had no reason to expect anyone in her house. I put my hand over her mouth just in case.

"Mama," I whispered.

She stared at me blankly. I took my hand away from her

mouth. "Oh, Anthony," she said, and her voice dripped with sadness.

"Mama," I said. "I want you to meet Hannah."

I stepped to the side and let Hannah step forward so that Berta could get as good a look at her as she could in little light. I saw Berta's eyes move up to Hannah's face. I wondered if she found it as lovely as I did. Hannah said, "Hello."

Berta ignored her and tried to sit up. "Don't get up, Mama," I said.

"What are you doing, Anthony?" she said. "You have to stop this madness."

"I just wanted to say I love you," I said.

Berta swiped at her dark bangs that fell across her forehead. "You need to stay here, Anthony," she said. "For me. There are people who need to see you."

"I can't do that," I said. "You know I can't do that."

"Please, Anthony, stop this. I beg you. Do it for the girl."

"I can't, Mama."

"Do it for your father's memory, then," she said.

"I'm sorry."

"Anthony," she said. "My baby. What has happened to you?"

"We have to go, Mama," I said. "I love you."

I leaned down and I kissed her a third time, this time on the cheek, and I felt her arms on my arms but we could not stay. I took Hannah again by the hand and we left my mother in the bed. I heard her rising behind us but we moved quickly down the stairs. We went out the front door this time and the street was deserted. There were no cops. We ran around the backyard and across the sandy lawns and between the other houses to where the truck waited for us.

I kept the headlights off until we reached the main road in front of the harbor. It had to be three in the morning and the streets were deserted. It wouldn't be long before the fishing village woke up. I parked the truck in front of the co-op. We climbed out of the truck. The air was redolent with fish and fuel and all the smells of the harbor. I could see Victor's place from here and I was tempted to go wake him but I did not dare risk it.

Hannah and I cut between the co-op and the cannery and out onto the wharves. The full moon was still out and in a sky of high clouds. Its milky light spread across the docks. In front of us the commercial boats sat in rows with their birds up high. I wondered if the *Lorrie Anne* was in.

"This way," I said.

We walked briskly past the boats to the far side of the harbor where all the small skiffs bobbed on the water. We were partway there, when I heard the siren. It was still in the distance, near Route 1, but it was growing louder.

"We have to go," I said, and Hannah looked behind us, toward the road, and for a moment she seemed frozen. I took her by the arm. "We can't," I said.

We broke into a run. I didn't even know if my skiff would be there. For all I knew they had taken it, anticipating we would need it, or they considered it evidence. But as we came charging on the wooden slats, past bail barrels and stacks of pallets, there it was, the little boat of mine, the boat that had once belonged to my father.

I helped Hannah in and I started the engine and to my relief there was plenty of gas. The sirens were closer now, and there were two of them, I thought, different pitches straining together. I backed the skiff out of its mooring and then piloted it through the other boats in the inner harbor. I pulled down on the throttle and took us past where the Cross Island ferry was docked for the night. Out on the main road, in front of the fish stores, I saw them now, streaming past, two then three cars, lights ablaze. No doubt if they looked up they would have seen our running lights. It wouldn't be long now.

We followed the buoys toward the mouth. The channel was wide and there was no other traffic and I pushed the small boat to its limit. Its nose rose into the air and the water streamed on either side of us. The wind blew our hair back and when I looked at Hannah I knew she was scared but I swear that part of her was enjoying this, the feel of the cool spray on our faces, the speed of the boat.

We passed the breakwater and entered the sound and I could not help but feel it. I whooped as loud as I could and I took Hannah's hand in mine and with my other one on the wheel, we raised our fists to the moon.

I knew they would look for us near the island first, so I headed straight out instead, deep into Long Island Sound. The ocean was empty at this time, other than a giant container ship, most likely bound for Boston, that we could see moving north, a gray mass at the edge of the horizon.

I cut the engine. In the moonlight we could see the full length of the mainland, dark and black except for the steady beam of the lighthouses, the one at Point Judith, the other over by Narragansett Bay. The small boat rose up and down in the mild chop. The sky was lightening. Dawn was not far away. I cleared space on the floor of the boat and I sat down, my back against the starboard side, and I motioned for Hannah to sit too. She sat next to me and she stretched her legs so that they ran along next to mine. Even not moving there was enough of a breeze that it whipped across the skiff. I lifted my arm and put it around her so she could rest her beautiful face on my shoulder.

"It's going to be okay," I said.

She cried. She cried hard and I knew she would and I let her, brushing her hair away from her forehead. "It'll be okay," I said again and again.

"I'm really scared."

"I know it," I said. I paused for a minute, and then I said, "I love you, Hannah."

"How do you know?"

"It's the only thing I know," I told her. "The rest of this, the rest of this is not real, you know what I mean? None of it matters. It's fake and it's stupid. Everyone else can have it. We don't need it. We have everything. We do. You have to trust me."

"I want to," she said between sobs. "I really do."

"Tell me you love me," I said.

She choked it out. "I love you."

I pulled her close. I listened for the Coast Guard cutters

but I did not hear them yet. They were fast boats. Most likely they were near the island, combing its shores, looking for us. I looked over the gunwale toward where the island was, though we were too far out to see any of it. The gentle rocking of the boat felt nice, and I said to Hannah, "You can sleep some if you want."

She didn't respond. We sat in silence and Hannah smushed her face into my shoulder and I played with her long hair. I ran my fingers through it. I looked up to the vastness of the blue-black sky. I couldn't see the moon anymore and there were no stars. There was nothing up there at all.

We must have fallen asleep. I don't remember drifting off, but when I woke I was disoriented. And then I felt the swell of the ocean and as my eyes adapted I saw that the September sun had climbed above the horizon. Dull and orange and not yet warm. Hannah was heavy on my arm. I turned to look at her and she stirred. I saw her blink and her eyes opened. She shivered against the morning.

"Hey," I said.

She rubbed her eyes. "What time is it?"

"I don't know," I said, though from the position of the sun it could not have been more than six in the morning. I lifted my tired arm away from her head and she leaned back against the boat and her arms fell to her side and she looked like a marionette that had been released. I stood up in the boat and looked around.

We had drifted to the west, that much I could tell. We could no longer see Galilee or Point Judith. In front of us, maybe two miles away, were the rocky shoals. Looking behind me I saw the tongue of land that was the easternmost tip of Long Island. I looked to the east, toward Cross Island, and with my sea-seasoned eyes I couldn't see the island, but I was able to see something else, not more than an abnormality at this point, something on the water. I knew right away what it was. By the way it moved. They couldn't have seen us yet, and maybe we were too small to show up on radar, but I couldn't know that. They were heading for us and their direction suggested purpose. The Coast Guard.

I didn't say anything to Hannah. We were on the open ocean and on the open ocean there was no place to hide. I went to the stern of the boat. I lifted the cushion that covered the battery and I felt down around its cap and to the wires that came off it. I found the one that controlled the bilge and I yanked it as hard as I could. It snapped off from the battery. I looked again at the ship coming toward us and I could make out the V of its bow. There was no mistaking it now, they knew where we were. They were still a mile away. But closing fast.

I glanced over at Hannah. And I will tell you this, but she had never been more remarkable. Maybe it was the early-morning light, but her green eyes sparkled like water trapping the sun, and her golden red hair fell on either side of that lovely face, framing her high cheekbones and her full lips. It took everything I had to turn away from her.

On my skiff the drainplug was on the bottom right of the stern. It always seems like there should be more to it. But I reached down and took it between my fingers and it was no more complex than letting the water out of a tub.

I rejoined Hannah and we sat on the floorboards. I heard the water before I saw it, spilling in and moving beneath us and I felt it too, though it's hard to describe how it felt. It was nothing more than a sudden heaviness in the boat.

I kissed her cheeks. I kissed her nose. Then her forehead. Then each of her eyes.

"I don't want to," she said.

"I love you," I said, and I began to cry.

The ocean was at our feet. It was as clear as broth, pale with flecks of green and blue. It lapped around our toes and it lifted up fishing hooks and other detritus on the floor of the boat. It covered our thighs and then washed over our laps. The boat listed to port. Hannah fell into me and I held her as best as I could. I put my arms around her wet clothes and I held her close. I heard the ship's engine and something inaudible coming over a loudspeaker. My skiff groaned with the weight of me and of Hannah and of the water. I put my hand over her mouth as we sank beneath the soft waves.

We fell apart underwater, like we did after we made love on a bed, when each of us collapsed to a different side. I had a sense of her drifting away from me, of the strands of her hair suspended, of the boat falling below us. I couldn't see a thing. It was dark and black and cold. It was also eerily peaceful, and I don't really know how to give this part words. The closest I can come is that it was like sleeping when you are awake. My eyes were open and I could not see anything but I was absolutely calm and my head was empty. I had no worries. No fears. My limbs felt loose and weightless.

Something passed in front of me. A whooshing sound. Then it came up and I felt arms around my body. I think I smiled dumbly. I did not resist. There were air bubbles in front of my face, like floating ball bearings. Then we rushed to the surface.

We broke through it and I began to choke. The pleasant feeling was all gone and my lungs ached and my body felt impossibly heavy. The man dragged me through the water. I saw the white hull of the large boat. Next thing I knew I was hooked to something and being lifted in the air. They brought me on the deck like a swordfish. They were all over me and I was coughing and spitting up ocean water. I couldn't see right. The sunlight looked strange and fuzzy.

"He's okay," a voice said.

I lay on the hard metal for what seemed like hours. Panting and gasping for air.

Gradually my sight came back. I tried to get up, and a voice said, "Just stay there."

I didn't move. Though I turned my head to the right and when I did, I saw Hannah, maybe five feet away, prone on her back like I was. Her face was as pale as flour and her lips looked shriveled. Her eyes were closed. A man straddled her chest and he was pressing on it. Over and over. Then he stood and he slammed something to the ground. I heard it hit.

"Fuck," he said. "Fuck."

After that, I fell asleep.

There were those days in the hospital, people coming in and out, Berta and Danny Pedroia and Detective Martini from the Rhode Island State Police who was the one who told me that Hannah had died. He said it so matter-of-factly and I suppose I knew it already, but it didn't go down any easier. It felt so unjust, my survival, and what bothered me the most was the finality of the separation. We either both should have lived, or we both should have died, and if only one of us wasn't going to make it, it should have been me. I was born to the sea and in a perfect world, I should have died in the sea for what I loved. As my father had.

There was my incarceration in the wing for the criminally insane. The anguished wails of my fellow inmates who I seemed to have nothing in common with besides this building we shared. I saw their faces, contorted and half-human, and in them I never saw myself. Their pain was so palpable, so real, that they needed to be kept from themselves. They were their own worst enemies, and whatever they might say about me, I was not one of them.

There were the hours and hours with the doctors, going

over the same material over and over. I held nothing back and I told them all I could. I told them everything they wanted to know, but mostly I told them about the love. The love I had for Hannah and the love she had for me. How most people live their whole lives and never know that kind of love. There is no adequate way to describe it and if you have not experienced it yourself you will never know what I am talking about. It's like having a bad case of the flu that doesn't go away, only it's pleasant. You know you have it, that it has infected every part of you, but you don't want it to go away. You want to succumb to it totally, let it course through your body and your mind like a virus. And the best part about it is that everything in this dark world makes sense for a time. The moon and the stars and the sun. The endless unforgiving ocean. The sand and the earth underneath your boots. It becomes real because of the touch, the feel, and the gaze of another person. You fall into each other and when you do there is no fear, no pain, no sorrow. There is just each other and somehow that is always enough.

The trial began on a Tuesday in October. The courtroom was stuffy and I remember that it was hard to breathe. The air was stale and still and I felt it in my throat. I stood to give my plea and I knew that all eyes were on me. They wanted to hear my voice, as if its very sound might answer all the questions they had about me. Danny Pedroia made me practice those words over and over. I tried to sound strong and confident, though I was neither of those things. I was indifferent at this point, to tell you the truth. I just wanted this over, the scrutiny. If I couldn't live with Hannah, I at least wanted to be able to live with her in mind, where no one could bother me.

I stood, and I said, "Innocent by reason of insanity."

I said it because I had to, not because I believed it. I knew what had happened and why it had happened. And other than the very end, when I was pulled out of the water against my will, I don't know that I would have done a thing differently. But there was no forum for me to say that, and I did not. I said those five words, enunciating them as clearly as I could, and then I sat down.

The first person the prosecution called was Victor. He

glanced at me quickly when he took the stand but the whole time he talked, he didn't once look in my direction. He wore his suit from the funeral home and he played with his mustache. The prosecutor, a sturdy-looking woman with shoulder-length brown hair, kept having to ask him to speak up. But Victor did pretty well. He didn't leave a whole lot out. He talked about the wake he did at the house, how he told me about the money. How I wanted it to use for college. He didn't mention anything about his wanting the money, too, but that was okay. I wasn't going to call him on it. Besides, the prosecutor went over this a dozen times, trying to show how clear-thinking I was. That I was making plans. Victor told them how we rode my skiff out and I insisted on going into the house alone. He told them how afterwards the only thing I would talk about was Hannah and when the woman prosecutor asked him if he thought that was odd, me talking only about the girl, Victor shook his head. "Nah," he said. "Tony always liked girls." Quite a few people in the courtroom chuckled at that and I even allowed myself a smile.

Sheriff Riker went next. He gave all the details of the scene at the house, of seeing Hannah's father on the floor next to the staircase. I tuned him out when he talked, to be honest. There was nothing new to what he said. Instead I scribbled on the paper in front of me, like I was taking notes. I also watched a long-haired woman in a flowing dress to my left, in the first row behind where the prosecutors sat. She had a big sketch pad and was drawing pictures of everyone in the courtroom. I liked to watch her work. She was fast and used colored pencils. She did a great one of the judge, and also a nice one of Danny Pedroia. She drew me a lot, and didn't seem to mind that I could see her doing it. But the one I liked the best was the one she did of Berta. I thought she captured her perfectly, her stoic face and the sweetness and depth of her sad eyes. If I could have, I would have asked her if I could have it.

They brought up Captain Alavares and he talked about how I didn't show up for his boat that time and left him a note. The prosecutor asked him if I had ever caused any trouble before, and he said, "Anthony was an able fisherman." It warmed my heart to hear him say it because I knew for Captain Alavares that this was the highest form of praise he could give.

Next they called old Terrence from the campground in Connecticut. I was surprised to see him and they cleaned him up for his big day in court. He limped up to the stand but otherwise he looked no worse for wear. He had a suit on. His face didn't show any sign of our fight, but then again it had been a couple of months. He said how I attacked him, and then took his car. He conveniently left out any part about his interest in Hannah and how that might of affected things. But I whispered all that to Danny Pedroia and when it was his turn he grilled him on it hard. Terrence didn't give in, though, and I realized he didn't have to. It was his word against mine and I was the one sitting over here.

The final witness the prosecution called was Hannah's mother, Irene Forbes. Everyone leaned forward in their seats as she made her way up the aisle and past me and to the stand. She wore a long black dress and heels, and the only hint of color came from a scarf around her neck that had a touch of red in it. When she sat down, the prosecution brought out a giant picture of Hannah and they propped it up so the jury could see it. It was slightly off center from where I sat, but I could see it nonetheless. It was only a shot of her face, and she was smiling, but there were her green eyes, and those freckles, and those full lips. I only looked at it for a moment. For in front of me was Irene Forbes, and in her face I saw more of Hannah than I saw in the photograph. She was a beautiful woman. The wrinkles coming off her eyes and her forehead seemed to accentuate her beauty, not detract from it. And in seeing her, I suppose I got a glimpse of what Hannah would have looked like had she lived, and the thought of this was almost too much for me to handle. I felt the tears coming and I fought them off as best I could. I looked away from her, toward the tall windows, and when I looked back she was staring right at me as she talked about her daughter. In her eyes I saw hatred. Pure naked hatred. And I couldn't blame her. She hadn't been with us. She couldn't have known the truth about Hannah and me. All she knew was what was in front of her. That Hannah was in the ground. And that I was here.

When the trial ended, the jury had found in our favor. Which only meant that I traded prison for a hospital. They drove me in a van to this place, and I got my first glimpse of its brick buildings and its manicured lawns, looking more like a college than anything else, except for the heavy fences with the swirls of barbwire at the top. There were the first few years in the buildings everyone calls the farm, and finally my move to this room on the third floor, this room that has become my home. This room that gives me the ocean in the distance when the leaves are off the trees.

I stand up from my desk. Outside my window the sun is coming up over the distant water. I take the notebook and I put it into a brown envelope. I write Dr. Mitchell on the front of it. Then I leave my room and walk those hallways that echo the sound of my shoes on the linoleum. I exit the building and walk across the green lawn to the administration building where Dr. Mitchell's big office is. The campus is deserted at this hour. I don't see anyone else except for a few orderlies over near the doorway to the farm smoking. They ignore me and I enter the administration building and at Dr. Mitchell's office, I place the envelope into the plastic bin next to his heavy wooden door.

You can't even understand how much I have hated you for what you did to my husband, and to my baby girl. During the trial it took all I had to look at you, and you looked so smug to me, like you didn't have a care in the world. And yet you took two lives. They may have been imperfect, but who knows what could have come if they had continued to live?

It was very hard for me to write this letter. It took a number of years for me to draw the strength I needed. In the end, I did it for Hannah. I wanted you to know the type of person she was, the type of person she might have been. She was so much more than an object for your sickness. She was a beautiful girl, and more beautiful inside than out. She could have had an amazing life. Sometimes I think about her in her thirties, married with children, happy, living in the kind of marriage that I always wanted. She would have learned from my mistakes, I think, and avoided many of the pitfalls. She would have been a great mother.

I don't hate you anymore. I haven't forgiven you either. And I won't ever try to understand what you did. But Hannah in her short life did not like hate. There was too much difficulty in her own home. She did everything she could do to bring light to the world.

My only hope is that somehow this letter gets through to you. That perhaps you can take something from it that will allow you to fully understand what you have done.

Dr. Mitchell and I sit across from one another. Between us is his leather-topped coffee table. This is October and outside the window I can see maintenance workers raking the bright yellow leaves of the great oak into big piles. On the table in front of us is my notebook.

"I want to give this back to you," Dr. Mitchell says.

"What did you think of it?"

He pauses. "I read it as a doctor, you have to know that. I think what I want to do Anthony, is give you some reading. Something I wrote."

"Oh?"

He leans over toward a side table and picks a big folder off the top of it. He puts it on the table in front of me.

"What is this?" I ask.

"Your file," he says.

"My file?"

"Everything we have learned about since you have been here. All my notes, notes from the other doctors. Test results. A summary of our findings."

"Why are you giving this to me?"

"You're right to ask. It's unusual. There are conditions under state law where patients can petition to see parts of their file, but seldom all of it. I agonized over this, Anthony. But after reading your account I came to the conclusion that it was the right thing to do. I think you will find the summary particularly useful. But you are welcome to read all of it. For all the obvious reasons, you cannot take it with you. You can stay here and read as long as you like. I will give you some privacy and will check back to see if you have any questions. Does that sound okay?"

I look down at the fat file on the table. Papers spill out of it. "All right, Dr. Mitchell," I say.

He stands up in front of me, smooths out the creases in his suit pants.

"I'll check in, Anthony," he says, and he leaves me alone.

I open the folder. There is a lot of paper, but of course I have been here a long time. In the back there are smaller, random pieces, handwritten, and as I flip through I also see charts and spreadsheets, no doubt the results of the dozens of tests I have taken over the years. In the front is the summary and as it turns out, it is all I need to read.

The subject, Anthony Lopes, came to Edgewood at eighteen years old after a successful insanity plea in the trial of a murder of another teen. With very little formal education, he had worked as a commercial fisherman before his arrest. Nevertheless, the subject is hyperintelligent, articulate, manipulative, and generally very lucid. He manifests all the obvious traits of narcissism. He can be very persuasive and charming. He will explain in great detail the nature of his crime though he shows very little outward emotion. There are no signs of auditory or visual hallucinations, as one would find in schizophrenia. It is difficult to ascertain, of course, but the subject may have had olfactory and tactile hallucinations.

It is the conclusion of this committee that the subject suffers from an acute, and rare, form of delusional disorder, erotomanic subtype. The subject has always maintained the victim of his murder had been in love with him, and that in fact, the two had been engaged in a loving relationship over the course of several months. While it is unusual for the erotomanic subtype to be present in males, some forensic samples do contain a preponderance of males. Many of these patients are associated with dangerous or assaultive behavior. There is no evidence to suggest that the victim was ever in love with the subject. In fact, the overwhelming evidence presented at the trial shows that the delusional disorder may have begun after the subject encountered the victim during a larceny. Following that event, the subject became convinced that the victim was in love with him and that he was in love with her. He developed elaborate rescue fantasies, consistent with erotomania. He then proceeded to act out these fantasies, abducting the victim at her family home and keeping her hostage for several weeks. After being apprehended, he managed to escape custody and reached the victim once again, abducting her a second time. This abduction resulted in her death, in what appeared to be an attempt at a murder/suicide.

What separates this case from others in the literature is the length of time of the delusion, and the fact that the delusion has survived the death of the object of the erotomania. There has been no transference to other victims. The subject has been repeatedly exposed to other patients of the opposite sex and has demonstrated no interest. Other than a brief trial of somatic treatment—the subject was given atypical antipsychotics for a six-month period with no sign of benefit—the treatment has been confined to individual psychotherapy. The subject's reticence to acknowledge a disorder and to view the events in question in any other light but the delusion has made treatment largely ineffective. The subject's intelligence and manipulative behavior have also impeded the therapy.

While the feeling of the committee is that the subject no longer presents a threat to himself or others, without progress in addressing the underlying delusion, there is nothing to recommend release.

I close the folder and stop reading. I lean back against the couch and I watch the men gathering leaves outside. It is a beautiful October day, and in the bright sunshine, they stand under the magnificent oak, now stripped bare and with stark limbs, and fill a cart attached to a tractor with all that yellow.

The door opens and Dr. Mitchell walks in. He comes over and takes his seat across from me.

"Do you need more time?" he asks.

I shake my head. "No."

"You understand the nature of our problem, then, Anthony."

I nod. "I think I do, Doctor."

Sometimes it is easier not to fight anymore. I decide to give them what they want, though I know enough to know that I will have to do it slowly, piece by piece. Any quicker and they will suspect that I am just trying to satisfy them and that they have given me the blueprint for doing so.

I do ask for one thing in return and on a beautiful autumn day that feels like summer, Dr. Mitchell grants my wish.

Two orderlies and a golf cart take me down to the southernmost edge of the campus. A guard is waiting at that gate and he opens it and we get out of the cart and walk through. We follow a bike path and when we reach the dunes, we walk along wooden boards and out to the beach.

It is wide-open Atlantic here, no islands or land visible when you look straight out. The orderlies wait for me while I walk across the empty beach to the water. My shoes sink into the sand but then I reach where the tide rolls in and the sand is hard here. I bend down and kick off my shoes. I go to the edge of the small whitecaps and then walk into them. The water is cold on my feet but I don't care. The waves lap against my legs and soak my pants. I look to the limitless horizon, to where the sky and the ocean become one.

It is so big and incomprehensible that it humbles me. I want nothing more than to dive into it, and swim for all I am worth. But I know the orderlies will be on me in a flash and I will accomplish nothing. No, I have to be patient, and work through this. I look down at the tide. I take the folded sheets of yellow legal paper out of my pocket. I lean down and place them on the water. They roll away from me on a small wave. The next small wave brings them back to me again. I watch them moving back and forth in the easy tide. The change is imperceptible but the tide is moving out. In an hour the folded paper will be thirty yards out. And maybe later it will get caught in the undertow. It will be swept out to sea.